JOSÉ EDUARD

José Eduardo Agualusa was born in Huambo, Angola, in 1960, and is one of the leading literary voices in Angola and the Portuguese-speaking world. His novel *Creole* was awarded the Portuguese Grand Prize for Literature, and *The Book of Chameleons* won the Independent Foreign Fiction Prize. Agualusa lives between Portugal, Angola and Brazil.

DANIEL HAHN

Daniel Hahn is an award-winning editor, writer and translator with over forty books to his name, including the translations of four previous novels by José Eduardo Agualusa. His most recent book is *The Oxford Companion to Children's Literature*.

ALSO BY JOSÉ EDUARDO AGUALUSA

Rainy Season
Creole
The Book of Chameleons
My Father's Wives

JOSÉ EDUARDO AGUALUSA

A General Theory of Oblivion

TRANSLATED FROM THE PORTUGUESE BY
Daniel Hahn

VINTAGE

1 3 5 7 9 10 8 6 4 2

Vintage
20 Vauxhall Bridge Road,
London SW1V 2SA

Vintage is part of the Penguin Random House group of companies
whose addresses can be found at global.penguinrandomhouse.com

 Penguin
Random House
UK

First published in Vintage in 2016
First published in hardback by Harvill Secker in 2015
First published with the title *Teoria Geral do Esquecimento*
in Portugal by Publicações Dom Quixote in 2012

penguin.co.uk/vintage

A CIP catalogue record for this book is available
from the British Library

ISBN 9780099593126

Grateful thanks to Grove Press for permission to reproduce Fernando
Pessoa's 'I feel sorry for the stars', *Fernando Pessoa & Co.: Selected Poems*,
translated by Richard Zenith, 1998

This book has been selected to receive financial assistance from English
PEN's "PEN Translates!" programme, supported by Arts Council England.
English PEN exists to promote literature and our understanding of it, to
uphold writers' freedoms around the world, to campaign against the
persecution and imprisonment of writers for stating their views, and to
promote the friendly co-operation of writers and the free exchange of ideas.
www.englishpen.org. The publication has also been assisted by a grant from
the Direção-Geral do Livro, dos Arquivos e das Bibliotecas / Portugal

Printed and bound by Clays Ltd, St Ives plc

Penguin Random House is committed to a sustainable future
for our business, our readers and our planet. This book is made
from Forest Stewardship Council® certified paper.

A GENERAL THEORY OF OBLIVION

FOREWORD

Ludovica Fernandes Mano died in Luanda, at the Sagrada Esperança clinic, in the early hours of 5 October 2010. She was eighty-five years old. Sabalu Estevão Capitango gave me copies of ten notebooks in which Ludo had been writing her diary, dating from the first years of the twenty-eight during which she had shut herself away. I also had access to the diaries that followed her release, as well as to a huge collection of photographs taken by the visual artist Sacramento Neto (Sakro) of Ludo's texts and the charcoal pictures on the walls of her apartment. Ludo's diaries, poems and reflections helped me to reconstruct the tragedies she lived through. They helped me, I believe, to understand her. In the pages that follow, I have made use of much of her first-hand accounts. What you will read is, however, fiction. Pure fiction.

OUR SKY IS YOUR FLOOR

Ludovica never liked having to face the sky. While still only a little girl, she was horrified by open spaces. She felt, upon leaving the house, fragile and vulnerable, like a turtle whose shell had been torn off. When she was very small – six, seven years old – she was already refusing to go to school without the protection of a vast black umbrella, whatever the weather. Neither her parents' annoyance nor the cruel mockery of the other children deterred her. Later on, it got better. Until what she called 'The Accident' happened and she started to look back on this feeling of primordial dread as something like a premonition.

After the death of her parents, Ludo lived in her sister's house. She rarely went out. She earned a little money giving Portuguese lessons to bored teenagers. Besides this, she read, embroidered, played the piano, watched television, cooked. When night fell, she would go over to the window and look into the darkness like someone leaning out over an abyss. Odete, irritated, would shake her head:

'What's the matter, Ludo? Scared of falling into the stars?'

Odete taught English and German at the high school. She loved her sister. She avoided travel so as not to leave Ludo by herself. She spent her holidays at home. Some of her friends praised her selflessness, others criticised her for being excessively indulgent. Ludo couldn't imagine living alone. And yet she worried that she had become a burden. She thought of the two of them as Siamese twins, joined at the navel. Herself, paralysed, almost dead, and the other, Odete, forced to drag her along wherever she went. She felt happy and she felt terrified when her sister fell in love with a mining engineer. His name was Orlando. A widower, childless. He had come to the Portuguese city of Aveiro to resolve some complicated issue to do with an inheritance. An Angolan, originally from Catete, he lived between Angola's capital and Dundo, a town run by the diamond company for which he worked. Two weeks after they'd met, quite by chance, in a patisserie, Orlando asked Odete to marry him. Expecting her to turn him down, being familiar with her reasons, he insisted that Ludo would go to live with them in Angola. The following month, they were set up in a huge apartment on the top floor of one of the most luxurious buildings in Luanda. The so-called Prédio dos Invejados – that is, the building of those who inspire envy.

The journey was hard for Ludo. She left home in a daze, under the effects of tranquillizers, moaning and protesting. She slept the whole flight. The following morning, she awoke to a routine similar to the one she'd had back home. Orlando owned a valuable library – thousands of titles, in Portuguese, French, Spanish, English and German, among which almost all the great classics of universal literature were to be found. Ludo had access to more books now, but also to less time, because she insisted on dispensing with the two maids and the cook, taking over all the domestic chores herself.

One evening, the engineer arrived home, carefully carrying a large cardboard box. He handed it to his sister-in-law:

'This is for you, Ludovica. To keep you company. You spend too much time alone.'

Ludo opened the box. Inside, looking fearfully at her, she found a little white newborn puppy.

'It's a male. A German Shepherd,' Orlando explained. 'They grow quickly. This one's an albino, rather unusual. He shouldn't get too much sun. What are you going to call him?'

Ludo didn't hesitate:

'Phantom!'

'Phantom?'

'Yes, he looks like a phantom. All white like that.'

Orlando shrugged his bony shoulders.

'Very well. Then Phantom he shall be.'

An elegant, anachronistic wrought-iron staircase climbed in a tight spiral from the drawing room up to the terrace. From there, your eyes could take in a good part of the city, the bay, the Ilha promontory, and off in the distance a long necklace of abandoned beaches fringed by the fine lacework of the waves. Orlando had taken advantage of the space to construct a garden. A bower of bougainvillea threw its scented lilac shade over the coarse brick floor. In one of the corners grew a pomegranate tree and several banana trees. Guests were often surprised:

'Bananas, Orlando? Is this a city garden or a backyard of a farm?'

The engineer would get annoyed. The banana trees reminded him of the large yard, hemmed in by adobe walls, where he had played as a boy. If it had been up to him, he would have planted mango trees too, and medlar trees, and lots of papaya plants. When he came home from the office, this garden was where he used to sit, a glass of whisky within arm's reach, a black cigarette alight between his lips, watching as night conquered the city. Phantom would be there with him. The puppy also loved the terrace. Ludo, meanwhile, refused to go up the stairs. In the first few months she did not even dare approach the windows.

'The African sky is much bigger than ours,' she explained to her sister. 'It crushes us.'

One sunny April morning, Odete came back from the high school to have her lunch. Chaos had broken out in the capital, and she was thrilled and frightened. Orlando was in Dundo. He arrived back that night, and shut himself away in the bedroom with his wife. Ludo could hear them arguing. Her sister wanted to leave Angola as quickly as possible:

'The terrorists, my love, the terrorists...'

'Terrorists? Never use that word in my house again.' Orlando never shouted. He whispered harshly, the sharp edge of his voice like a blade against the throats of his interlocutors. 'These so-called terrorists are fighting for the freedom of my country. I am Angolan. I will not leave.'

Turbulent days passed. Demonstrations, strikes, rallies. Ludo closed the windows to prevent the apartment from being filled with the laughter of the people on the streets, which burst into the air like fireworks. Orlando, the son of a trader from Minho who'd settled in Catete in the early years of the century, and a Luandan mestiza who'd died in childbirth, had never nurtured family connections. However, one of his cousins, Vitorino Gavião, showed up again around this time. He had spent five months living in Paris, occupying himself with drink, women, plotting, and writing poems on paper napkins in the bistros that were frequented by exiles from Portugal and Africa, thereby acquiring the aura of a romantic revolutionary. He entered their house like a tempest, disordering the books in the bookcase, the glasses on the dresser, and unsettling Phantom. The puppy would chase around after him at a safe distance, barking and growling.

'The comrades want to speak to you, damn it!' shouted Vitorino, levelling a punch at Orlando's shoulder. 'We're negotiating a provisional government. We need good men.'

'Could be,' admitted Orlando. 'Actually, we have plenty of good men. What we're short of is good sense.'

Then he paused. Yes, he said, quietly now, the country could use the experience he had gathered. But he feared the more extremist currents at the heart of the movement. He understood the necessity for greater social justice, but the communists, who were threatening to nationalise everything, alarmed him. Expropriating private property. Expelling the whites. Knocking out all the petite bourgeoisie's teeth. He, Orlando, took pride in having a perfect smile, and he had no desire for dentures. His cousin laughed, attributing their verbal excesses to the euphoria of the moment, then complimented him on the whisky and poured himself some more. This cousin with a sphere of curly hair like Jimi Hendrix, a flowery shirt open across his sweating chest, alarmed the sisters.

'He talks like a black!' said Odete, accusingly. 'And besides, he stinks. Whenever he comes over, he infects the whole house.'

Orlando became enraged. He left, slamming the door behind him. He returned in the evening, drier, sharper, a man with a close kinship to a thorn bush. He went up to the terrace, Phantom with him, took a pack of cigarettes, a bottle of whisky, and there he stayed. He returned when night was drawing in, bringing the darkness with him, and a strong smell of alcohol and tobacco. He stumbled over his own feet, shoving into the furniture, with harsh whispers against this whole fucking life.

The first gunshots signalled the start of the big farewell parties. Young people were dying in the streets, waving flags, and meanwhile the settlers danced. Rita, their neighbour in the apartment next door, traded Luanda for Rio de Janeiro. On her last night, she invited two hundred friends round for a dinner that went on till daybreak.

'Whatever we can't drink we'll leave for you,' she said to Orlando, pointing at the pantry stacked high with cases of the finest Portuguese wines. 'Drink them. The important thing is that there mustn't be anything left over for the communists to celebrate with.'

Three months later, the apartment block was almost empty. Ludo, meanwhile, didn't know where to put so many bottles of wine, crates of beer, tins of food, hams, pieces of salt cod, and kilos of salt, sugar and flour, not to mention the endless supply of cleaning and hygiene products. Orlando had received from one friend – a collector of sports cars – a Chevrolet Corvette and an Alfa Romeo GTA. Another had given him the keys to his apartment.

'I've never been a lucky man,' Orlando complained to the two sisters, and it was not clear whether he was being ironic or speaking in earnest. 'Just when I start collecting cars and apartments, the communists show up wanting to take everything away from me.'

Ludo would turn on the radio and the revolution would come into the house. '*It's the power of the people that is the cause of all this chaos,*' one of the most popular singers of the moment kept repeating. '*Hey, brother,*' sang another, '*love your brother / Don't look to see what his colour is / Just see him as Angolan / With the Angolan people united / Independence will soon be here.*' Some of the tunes didn't really go with the words. It was as though they were stolen from songs of another age, ballads that were sad like the light of an ancient dusk. Leaning out of the window, half hidden behind the curtains, Ludo could see the trucks pass by, loaded up with men. Some of them were flying flags. Others had banners with slogans:

Full Independence!
500 years of colonial oppression are enough!
We want the Future!

The demands all ended in exclamation marks. The exclamation marks got mixed up with the machetes the protesters were carrying. There were also machetes shining on the flags and the banners. Some of the men were carrying one in each hand. They were holding them up high. They were striking the blades against one another in a mournful clamour.

One night, Ludo dreamed that beneath the streets of the city, under the respectable mansions in the lower town, there stretched an endless network of tunnels. The roots of the trees wound their way, unimpeded, down through the vaults. There were thousands of people living underground, sunk deep in mud and darkness, feeding themselves on whatever the bourgeoisie tossed into the sewers. Ludo was walking amid the throng. The men were waving machetes. They were striking their blades against one another and the noise echoed down the tunnels. One of them approached, brought his dirty face right up close to the Portuguese woman's face and smiled. He whispered in her ear, in a voice that was deep and sweet:

'Our sky is your floor.'

LULLABY FOR A SMALL DEATH

Odete insisted that they leave Angola. Her husband responded with muttered, harsh words. The women could go if they
wanted. Let the settlers set sail. Nobody wanted them here.
A cycle was being completed. A new time was beginning. Come
sun or storm, the Portuguese would not be lit by the light of
the future, nor lashed by wild hurricanes. The more he and
Odete whispered, the angrier the engineer got. He could spend
hours enumerating the crimes committed against the Africans,
the mistakes, the injustices, the disgraces, until his wife gave
up and shut herself away in the guest bedroom in tears. It
was a huge surprise when he arrived home, two days before
Independence, and announced that in a week's time they would
be in Lisbon. Odete opened her eyes wide:

'Why?'

Orlando sat down in one of the living room armchairs. He
pulled off his tie, unbuttoned his shirt and, finally, in a gesture
quite unlike him, took off his shoes and put his feet up on the
little coffee table.

'Because we can. We can go, now.'

The next night the couple went out for yet another farewell party. Ludo waited for them to come home – reading, knitting, till two in the morning. She went to bed worried, and she slept badly. She got up at seven, put on a dressing gown, called out to her sister. Nobody answered. She was certain some tragedy must have befallen them. She waited an hour before looking for their address book. First she called the Nuneses, the couple who had organised the previous night's party. One of the servants answered. The family had gone off to the airport. Mr Orlando the engineer and his wife had indeed been at the party, that was right, but they hadn't stayed long. He'd never seen Mr Orlando in such a good mood. Ludo thanked him and hung up. She opened the address book again. Odete had scratched out in red ink the names of the friends who had left Luanda. Few remained. Only three answered, and none of them knew a thing. One of them, a maths teacher at the Salvador Correia high school, promised to phone a policeman friend of his. He would call back as soon as he had any information.

Hours passed. There was gunfire. First some isolated shots and then the intense crackle of dozens of automatic weapons. The telephone rang. A man who seemed still young, with a Lisbon accent, who sounded like he came from a good family, asked if he might speak to Miss Odete's sister.

'What's happened?'

'Take it easy, ma'm, we just want the stones.'

'The stones?'

'You know perfectly well what I'm talking about. Give us your jewels and I give you my word of honour we'll leave you in peace. Nothing's going to happen to you. Not to you or to

14

your sister. The two of you can go back to the big city on the next plane if that's what you want.'

'What have you done with Odete and my brother-in-law?'

'The old man has been behaving irresponsibly. There are some people who mistake stupidity for courage. I'm an officer in the Portuguese army and I don't like people trying to trick me.'

'What have you done with her? What have you done with my sister?'

'We don't have much time. This can end well or it can end badly.'

'I don't know what you mean, I swear I don't know...'

'Look, you wanna see your sister again? Keep nice and quiet at home, don't try to tell anyone. As soon as things have calmed down a bit we'll come by your apartment to fetch the stones. You hand over the package and we'll release Miss Odete.'

He said this and hung up. Night fell. Bullet-lines streaked across the sky. Explosions shook the windowpanes. Phantom hid behind one of the sofas. He was whimpering quietly. Ludo felt dizziness, felt agony. She ran to the bathroom and threw up in the toilet, then sat down on the floor, trembling. As soon as she had recovered her strength, she went straight over to Orlando's study, which she entered only once every five days to dust and sweep the floor. The engineer was very proud of his desk, a solemn, fragile piece of furniture he had bought from a Portuguese antiques dealer. Ludo tried to open the first drawer. She couldn't do it. She went to fetch a hammer and split it open in three furious blows. She found a pornographic magazine. She pushed it aside, disgusted, only to find a wad

15

of hundred-dollar bills underneath, and a pistol. She held the gun with both hands. She felt its weight. She stroked it. This was what men used to kill each other. A dense, dark instrument, almost alive. She turned the apartment upside down. She found nothing. Finally she stretched out on one of the living room sofas and fell asleep. She awoke with a start. Phantom was tugging at her skirt. He was growling. A sea breeze gently lifted the fine lace curtains. There were stars floating in the void. The silence amplified the darkness. A wave of voices was coming up the corridor. Ludo got up, and she walked, barefoot, to the front door and looked through the spyhole. Outside, by the elevators, there were three men arguing in low voices. One of them pointed towards her – towards the door – with a crowbar:

'A dog, I'm sure of it. I heard a dog barking.'

'What are you talking about, Minguito?' He was challenged by a tiny, very thin man dressed in a military dolman that was too wide and too long. 'There's nobody here. The settlers have gone. Go on. Knock that piece of shit down.'

Minguito walked up. Ludo stepped back. She heard the blow and, without stopping to think, she returned it, a violent blow against the wood that left her breathless. Silence. Then a shout:

'Who's there?'

'Go away.'

Laughter. The same voice:

'There's one left behind! What's up, ma, did they forget you?'

'Please, go away.'

'Open the door, ma. We only want what belongs to us. You

people have been stealing from us for five hundred years. We've come to take what's ours.'

'I have a gun. Nobody is coming in.'

'Lady, just take it easy. You give us your jewels, a bit of money, and we'll leave. We've got mothers, too.'

'No. I'm not opening up.'

'OK, Minguito, knock it down.'

Ludo ran to Orlando's study. She grabbed the pistol, walked back, and pointed it at the front door, squeezing the trigger. She would remember the moment of the gunshot day after day for the next thirty-five years. The bang, the slight jump of the gun. The quick pain in her wrist.

What would her life have been like without that one moment?

'Argh, I'm bleeding. Ma, you've killed me.'

'Trinitá! Pal, are you hurt?'

'Get out of here, move it...'

Gunshots out in the street, very close. Shots attract other shots. Fire a bullet in the air and it will soon be joined by dozens of others. In a country in a state of war, any bang is enough. A faulty car exhaust. A rocket. Anything. Ludo went over to the door. She saw the hole made by the bullet. She put her ear to the wood. She heard the muted gasping of the wounded man:

'Water, ma. Help me...'

'I can't... I can't.'

'Please, lady. I'm dying.'

The woman opened the door, shaking badly, never releasing her grip on the pistol. The burglar was sitting on the floor, leaning against the wall. Were it not for the thick black beard, he might have been taken for a child. A childlike little face, covered in sweat, with big eyes that gazed at her without any bitterness.

'Such bad luck, such bad luck, I'm not going to see Independence.'

'I'm sorry, I didn't mean it.'

'Water. I'm so terribly thirsty.'

Ludo threw a frightened glance down the corridor.

'Come inside. I can't leave you here.'

The man dragged himself in, groaning. He moved across the floor, leaving behind a second shadow on the wall. One darkness unsticking itself from another. Ludo stepped in that shadow with her bare feet and slipped.

'Oh God!'

'I'm sorry, grandma. I'm messing up your house.'

Ludo closed the door. She locked it. She headed for the kitchen, took some cold water from the fridge, filled a glass and returned to the living room. The man drank greedily.

'What I really need is just a little glass of fresh air.'

'I have to call a doctor.'

'It's not worth it. They'd kill me anyway. Sing me a song, grandma?'

'What?'

'Sing. Sing me a song, something soft like cotton wool.'

Ludo thought of her father, humming popular old ditties from Rio de Janeiro to put her to sleep. She placed the pistol on the wooden floor tiles, knelt down, took the burglar's tiny hands in hers, brought her mouth close to his ear, and sang.

She sang for a long time.

No sooner had the dawn light woken the house than Ludo summoned all her courage, gathered the dead man in her arms, without too much effort, and carried him out to the terrace. She went to fetch a shovel. She dug a narrow grave in one of the flowerbeds, amid the yellow roses.

Months earlier, Orlando had started to build a small swimming pool on the terrace. The war had stopped the work. The workers had left piles of bricks, and bags of cement and sand leaning against the walls. The woman dragged some of the material down the stairs. She unlocked the front door and went out. She began to construct a wall in the hallway, cutting off the apartment from the rest of the building. She spent the whole morning doing it. It was not until the wall was ready, and she had smoothed down the cement, that she felt hungry and thirsty. She heated up some soup, sat at the kitchen table and ate slowly. She gave some leftover roast chicken to the dog.

'Now it's just you and me.'

The animal came over and licked her fingers.

The blood had dried by the front door, forming a dark stain. There were footprints leading from there to the kitchen. Phantom licked them. Ludo pushed him away. She went to fetch a bucket of water, some soap and a brush, and she cleaned it all up. Then she took a hot shower. As she was stepping out of the tub the phone rang. She picked it up.

'Things got complicated. We weren't able to come by yesterday to collect the goods. We'll be coming over soon.'

Ludo put down the phone without answering. It rang again. Then it let up for a moment, but as soon as the woman turned her back it resumed its shrieking, nervously insisting on her attention. Phantom came out of the kitchen. He began to run in circles, barking fiercely at each jingling noise. Suddenly he jumped onto the table, knocking over the handset. The fall was violent. Ludo shook the black box. Something inside had come loose. She smiled.

'Thank you, Phantom. I don't think this will be bothering us any more.'

Outside in the turbulent night, rockets and mortars exploded. Cars hooted their horns. Looking out of the window, the Portuguese woman saw the crowd making its way along the roads, filling the squares with an urgent, desperate euphoria. She shut herself in her room. She stretched out on the bed. She buried her face in the pillow. She tried to imagine herself very far away, in the safety of her old house in Aveiro, watching old movies on television while sipping tea and crunching on pieces of toast. She couldn't do it.

SOLDIERS WITHOUT FORTUNE

The two men were struggling to hide their nerves. They had thin beards and long, dishevelled hair. They wore brightly coloured shirts, bell-bottomed trousers and jackboots. Benjamin, the younger one, was whistling loudly as he drove. Jeremias – Carrasco – was sitting beside him, chewing on a cigar. They passed flatbed trucks transporting soldiers. The lads waved to them, drowsily, making a V for victory. The two men responded the same way.

'Cubans!' growled Jeremias. 'Damn communists.'

They parked the car outside the Prédio dos Invejados and got out. A beggar was blocking the entrance.

'Morning, comrades.'

'And what the hell do you want?' Jeremias scolded him. 'You've come to the white men to ask for money? Those days are over. In an independent Angola, at the front line of socialism in Africa, there's no place for beggars. Beggars get their heads cut off.'

He shoved him aside and went into the building. Benjamin followed. They called the elevator and rode it up to the eleventh

23

floor. They found themselves, to their surprise, stopped short by the recently built wall.

'What the hell? This country's gone mad!'

'Is this really the place? Are you sure?'

'You're asking me if I'm sure?' Jeremias smiled. He pointed at the door opposite. 'Here, in Eleven-E, this is where Ritinha lived. Best legs in Luanda. Finest ass. You're lucky you never met Ritinha. Any man who met her could never look at another woman without a vague feeling of disappointment and bitterness. Like the African sky. *If they make me leave this place, God, where would I go?*'

'I understand, captain. What should we do?'

'We'll fetch a pickaxe and break through the wall.'

They returned to the elevator and went back down. The beggar was waiting for them, accompanied by five armed men.

'Those are the ones, comrade Monte.'

The man called Monte stepped forward. He addressed Jeremias in a voice that was certain, powerful, that contrasted with the leanness of his body:

'Would you mind rolling up the sleeve of your shirt, comrade? Yes, your right shirtsleeve. I want to see your wrist...'

'And why would I do that?'

'Because I'm asking you nicely, all polite like a perfumer.'

Jeremias laughed. He pulled back his shirtsleeve to reveal a tattoo: *Audaces Fortuna Juvat.*

'You wanted to see this?'

'Just that, captain. Seems your luck has run out. Also, I do feel that two white men out on the street wearing Portuguese army boots in these troubled times seems a little too bold.'

He turned to two of the armed men and ordered them to fetch some rope to tie up the Portuguese mercenaries. They bound their hands behind their backs and pushed them into a very beaten-up Toyota Corolla. One of the men rode shotgun. Monte was at the wheel. The others followed behind in a military jeep. Benjamin dropped his head between his knees, unable to hold back the tears. Jeremias was annoyed, and nudged him with his shoulder:

'Take it easy. You're a Portuguese soldier.'

Monte butted in:

'Leave the kid alone. You shouldn't have brought him to our country. As for you, sir, you are no more than a whore in the pay of American imperialism. You ought to be ashamed.'

'And what about the Cubans? Aren't they mercenaries, too?'

'Our Cuban companions didn't come to Angola for the money. They came because of their convictions.'

'And I stayed in Angola because of my convictions. I'm fighting for Western civilisation, against Soviet imperialism. I'm fighting for Portugal's survival.'

'Bullshit. I don't believe that. You don't believe that, even your mother wouldn't believe that. Talking of which, what were you doing in Rita's building?'

'Wait, you know Rita?'

'Rita Costa Reis? Ritinha? Great legs. Best legs in Luanda.'

They chatted happily about Angolan women. Jeremias did fancy the Luandan ones, however, he added, there wasn't a woman in the world who could match the mulatta women of Benguela. Then Monte recalled Riquita Bauleth, born into one of the oldest families in Moçâmedes, named Miss Portugal in 1971. Jeremias concurred. Yes, Riquita – he would give his life just to be able to wake up one morning in the light of those dark eyes. The man sitting beside Monte interrupted the conversation:

'This is the place, commander. We're here.'

They had left the city behind. A high wall marked out a wide, open area. Baobab trees at the far end, and then a spotless blue horizon. They got out of the car. Monte untied the two mercenaries. He straightened up.

'Captain Jeremias Carrasco... Carrasco, as in "executioner"? Well, I'm assuming that's got to be a nickname... You are guilty of countless atrocities. You tortured and murdered dozens of Angolan nationalists. Some of our comrades would like to see you in a courtroom. But I don't think we ought to be wasting our time with trials. The people have found you guilty already.'

Jeremias smiled.

'The people? Bullshit. I don't believe that. You don't believe that, even your mother wouldn't believe that. Let us go free and I'll give you a fistful of diamonds. Good stones. You can leave this place and make a new life anywhere else. You'll be able to get any woman you want.'

'Thank you. I have no intention of leaving, and the only woman I want I've got at home. Have a good journey, and enjoy yourself where you're going...'

Monte walked over to the car. The soldiers pushed the Portuguese men up against the wall. They took a few steps back. One of them pulled a pistol from his belt, and in a movement that was almost absent-minded, almost annoyed, he pointed it and fired three times. Jeremias Carrasco was lying on his back. He saw the birds flying high in the sky. He noticed an inscription in red ink on the bloodstained, bullet-pocked wall:

The struggle continues.

THE SUBSTANCE OF FEAR

*I am afraid of what's outside the window, of the air
that arrives in bursts, and the noise it brings with it.
I am scared of mosquitos, the myriad of insects I don't
know how to name. I am foreign to everything, like
a bird that has fallen into the current of a river.*

*I don't understand the languages I hear outside, the
languages the radio brings into the house. I don't
understand what they're saying, not even when they
sound like they're speaking Portuguese, because this
Portuguese they are speaking is no longer mine.*

Even the light seems strange to me.

Too much light.

Certain colours ought not to occur in a healthy sky.

I am closer to my dog than to those people out there.

31

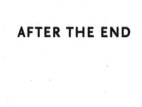

AFTER THE END

After the end, time slowed down. At least that was how it seemed to Ludo. On 23 February 1976 she wrote, in the first of her diaries:

> *Nothing happened today. I slept.*
> *While asleep I dreamed that I was sleeping.*

> *Trees, little animals, a multitude of insects were sharing their*
> *dreams with me. There we all were, dreaming in chorus, like*
> *a crowd in a tiny room, exchanging ideas and smells and*
> *caresses. I remember I was both a spider advancing towards its*
> *prey and the fly caught in the web of that spider. I felt flowers*
> *blossoming in the sun, breezes carrying pollen. I awoke and*
> *was alone. If, while we are asleep, we can dream of sleeping,*
> *can we then, when awake, awaken within a more lucid reality?*

One morning she got up, turned on the tap and the water didn't come out. She was scared. It occurred to her for the first time that she might spend long years shut away in the apartment. She took an inventory of what was in the pantry. She wouldn't need to worry about salt. She also found enough flour for several months, as well as bags and bags of beans, packets of sugar, cases of wine and soft drinks, dozens of tins of sardines, tuna and sausages.

That night it rained. Ludo opened an umbrella and went up onto the terrace, carrying empty bottles, buckets and basins. Early the next morning she cut the bougainvillea and the ornamental flowers. She put a handful of lemon pips in the flowerbed where she had buried the tiny burglar. Four other flowerbeds were used for sowing corn and beans. In another five, she planted her last remaining potatoes. One of the banana trees had borne a huge bunch. She pulled off a few bananas and carried them to the kitchen. She showed them to Phantom:

'See? Orlando planted the banana trees so they would produce memories. They're going to stop us going hungry. Or rather, they'll stop me going hungry, I can't imagine you're too keen on bananas.'

The next day, the water was back in the taps. From then on it would often fail, as would the electricity, till finally it went for good. In the first few weeks, the blackouts were more of a problem than the interruptions to the water supply. She missed the radio. She had liked hearing the international news bulletins on the BBC and Radiodifusão Portuguesa. She'd listened to the Angolan stations, too, even if the constant speeches against colonialism, neo-colonialism and the reactionary forces annoyed her. The radio was a magnificent piece of equipment, in a wooden casing, art deco style, with ivory buttons. Press one of the buttons and it lit up like a city. Ludo would turn the knobs in search of voices. Fragments of sentences would come to her in French, English or some obscure African language:

... *Israeli commandos rescue airliner hostages at Entebbe...*

... *Mao Tse-tung est mort...*

... *Combatants de l'indépendance aujourd'hui victorieux...*

... *Nzambe azali bolingo mpe atonda na boboto...*

Besides this, there was the record player. Orlando collected LPs of chansons. Jacques Brel, Charles Aznavour, Serge Reggiani, Georges Brassens, Léo Ferré. The Portuguese woman would listen to Brel as the sea swallowed up the light. The city falling asleep, and her struggling to remember names. A patch of sun still burning. And the night, bit by bit, time stretching out aimlessly. Body weary, and the night turning from blue to blue. Tiredness pressing on her kidneys. Seeing herself as a queen, believing that someone, someplace, could be waiting for her just as one awaits a queen. But there was no one, not anywhere in the world, waiting for her. The city falling asleep and the birds like waves, and the waves like birds, and the women like women, and her not at all sure that women are the future of Man.

One afternoon, she was woken by a resounding clamour of voices. In a panic she got up, imagining that the house was about to be invaded. The living room was adjacent to Rita Costa Reis's apartment. She pressed her ear to the wall. Two women, one man, several children. The man's voice was big, silky, lovely to listen to. They were talking to one another in one of those enigmatic, melodic languages that she would sometimes hear on the radio. The odd word would come loose from the pack and leap about, like a coloured ball bouncing back and forth inside her brain:

Bolingô. Bisô. Matindi.

The Prédio dos Invejados livened up as new residents began to arrive. People coming from the slum housing on the outskirts of Luanda, country folk who had just arrived in the city, Angolans lately returned from neighbouring Zaire, and real Zaireans too. None of them were used to living in an apartment block. One morning, really early, Ludo looked out the bedroom window to find a woman urinating on the balcony of 10-A. On the balcony of 10-D, five chickens were watching the sunrise. The back of the building overlooked a large courtyard, which only months before had still been used as a car park. Tall blocks, to the side and in front, hemmed the space in. The flora had run wild and launched itself over the entire area. There was water rising from some chasm in the centre, flowing freely, then finally petering out amid the heaps of rubbish and mud by the walls of the buildings. That was the place where a lagoon had once spread itself out. Orlando liked to remember the thirties, when he, then just a boy, would play with his friends in the tall grass. They'd find the skeletal remains of crocodiles and hippos. Lion skulls.

Ludo witnessed the revival of the lagoon. She even saw the return of the hippos (the one hippo, if we're to be completely objective). This happened many years later. We will get there. In the months that followed Independence, the woman and the dog shared tuna and sardines, sausages and chorizos. Once the tins had been emptied, they moved on to eating bean soups and rice. By this point, whole days passed with no electricity.

Ludo started making small bonfires in the kitchen. First she burned the boxes, the bits of paper of no use, the dry branches of the bougainvillea. Then the pieces of furniture that served no purpose. When she removed the crossbars from the double bed, she found, under the mattress, a small leather purse. She opened it and, feeling no surprise, watched as dozens of small stones rolled out onto the floor. After burning beds and chairs, she started to pull up the floor tiles. The dense, heavy wood burned slowly, with a fine flame. At first she used matches. Once those had run out, she moved on to one of the magnifying glasses Orlando had used to study his collection of foreign stamps. She would wait for the sun, at around ten in the morning, to flood the kitchen floor with light. Obviously, she could only cook on sunny days.

The hunger came. For weeks, weeks as long as months, Ludo barely ate. She fed Phantom on flour porridge. Nights merged into days. She would wake to find the dog watching over her with fierce eagerness. She would fall asleep and feel his burning breath. She went to the kitchen to fetch a knife, the one with the longest blade there was, the sharpest one, and took to carrying it around, attached to her waist like a sword. She would lean over the animal as he slept. Several times, she brought the knife to his throat.

It got dark, it got light, and it was the same void with no beginning and no end. At some indeterminate moment she heard, coming from the terrace, a loud rustling. She rushed upstairs and found Phantom devouring a pigeon. She approached, resolved to tear off a piece. The dog drove his paws into the ground and showed his teeth. Blood, thick and nocturnal, with feathers and flesh still clinging to it, covered his muzzle. The woman drew back. It occurred to her to prepare a very simple trap. A box turned upside down, tilted precariously, resting on a piece of kindling. A piece of thread tied to the twig. In the shade, two or three diamonds. She waited for more than two hours, crouched low, hidden behind the umbrella, until a pigeon touched down on the terrace. The bird approached with the little tottering steps of a drunk. It backed away. It beat its wings and flew off, lost in the brightly lit sky. Not long afterwards, it returned. This time it walked around the trap, pecked at the thread, moved forwards into the shade of the box. Ludo pulled the thread. That afternoon she successfully trapped two more pigeons. She cooked them and recovered her strength. In the months that followed, she caught many more.

For a long time there was no rain. Ludo watered the flower-beds with the water that had accumulated in the swimming pool. Finally, there was a rip in the cold curtain of low-hanging clouds, which in Luanda they call *cacimbo*, and the rain came down again. The corn grew. The bean plants yielded flowers and beans. The pomegranate tree was filled with red fruit. Around that time, the pigeons in the city's sky became more scarce. One of the last ones to fall into her trap had a ring wrapped around its right leg. Attached to the ring, Ludo found a little plastic cylinder. She opened it and discovered a slip of paper, rolled up like a raffle ticket. She read the line that was written in lilac-coloured ink, in a small firm hand:

Tomorrow. Six o'clock, usual place. Be very careful. I love you.

She rolled the piece of paper back up and replaced it in the cylinder. She hesitated. Hunger gnawed at her stomach. And the pigeon had swallowed one or two of the stones. There were not many left, some of them too big to serve as bait. On the other hand, the note intrigued her. She felt powerful all of a sudden. The fate of a couple was there, in her hands, pulsing in pure terror. She held it firmly, this winged destiny, and threw it back at the big, wide sky. She wrote in her diary:

> *I'm thinking about the woman waiting for the pigeon. She doesn't trust the mail – or is there no longer any mail? She doesn't trust the telephone – or have the phones stopped working now? She doesn't trust people, that's for sure. Humanity hasn't worked out too well. I can see her holding the pigeon, not knowing that before her I'd already held it, trembling, in my own hands. The woman wants to run away. I don't know what it is she wants to run away from. From this country that is coming apart, from a suffocating marriage, from one of those futures that squeeze your feet like someone else's shoes? I thought to add a little note of my own: 'Kill the Messenger'. Yes, for if she killed the pigeon she would find a diamond. Or she would read the note and return the pigeon to the pigeon house. At six in the morning she would go to meet a man I imagine to be tall, with controlled movements and an attentive heart. He is lit by a vague sadness (this man) as he prepares for their flight. A flight that will make him a traitor to the fatherland. He will wander the world, taking support from the love of a woman, but he will never be able to fall asleep at night without first bringing his hand to his left breast.*

> *The woman notices the gesture.*

The man will shake his head – no. Nothing. It's nothing.
How to explain that what hurts is the childhood he has lost?

Leaning out of the bedroom window, she would see, on the drawn-out Saturday mornings, one of the neighbour-women on the veranda of 10-D, pounding corn. Then she would see her mashing up the cassava paste. Preparing and grilling fish or, at other times, fat chicken legs. The air would be filled with a thick, scent-heavy smoke that would rouse her appetite. Orlando used to like Angolan food. Ludo, however, had always refused to cook black people's things. She regretted that very much. These days, what she most fancied was to eat grilled meat. She started to watch the chickens that lived on the veranda, scratching away, as the day broke, at the first grains of sunlight. She waited till one Sunday morning. The city slept. She leaned out of the window and lowered a piece of string, with a slip noose at the end, down to the veranda of 10-D. About fifteen minutes later she managed to loop the neck of a huge black rooster. She gave a sharp tug, and brought it up quickly. To her surprise, the animal was still alive (though only barely) when she set it on the bedroom floor. She drew the knife from her waist, she was going to slit its throat – then a sudden flash of inspiration stopped her. There would be enough corn for the next few months, as well as beans and bananas. With a rooster and a hen she could start breeding. It would be good to eat fresh eggs every week. She lowered the string again and this time she managed to loop one of the hens by a leg. The wretched bird struggled, an appalling uproar, feathers and down and dust flying. A moment later the building was woken by the neighbour's screams:

'Thieves! Thieves!'

Then, having ascertained the impossibility of anyone scaling the smooth walls to get to the veranda and steal the poultry, the woman's accusations were transformed into a terrified wailing:

'Witchcraft... Witchcraft...'

Then, straight away, with total certainty:

'A Kianda... A Kianda...'

Ludo had heard Orlando talk about a sea goddess called the Kianda. Her brother-in-law had tried to explain to her the difference between Kiandas and mermaids:

'A Kianda is a being, an energy capable of good or evil. This energy is expressed through the coloured lights that come from the water, through the waves of the sea and the raging of the winds. Fishermen pay her tribute. When I was a child and I used to play by the lagoon, the one behind this very building, I was always finding offerings. Sometimes the Kianda would kidnap somebody as they strolled past. People would reappear days later, very far away, beside some other lagoon or river, or on some beach. That used to happen a lot. After a certain point, the Kianda began to be represented in the form of a mermaid. She was transformed into a mermaid, but kept her original powers.'

Thus it was, with a vulgar theft and a stroke of luck, that Ludo began a small run of poultry-breeding on her terrace, while simultaneously contributing to strengthening the Luandans' belief in the presence and powers of the Kianda.

43

CHE GUEVARA'S MULEMBA TREE

CHE GUEVARA'S MULEMBA TREE

*Down in the yard, where the lagoon once rose up, there is an
enormous tree. I have discovered, by consulting a book from
the library about Angolan flora, that it is a 'mulemba' (Ficus
thonninglii). In Angola, it is considered the Royal Tree, or
Word Tree, because the tribal chiefs and elder women often
meet in its shade to discuss the problems of the tribe. The
highest branches almost reach the windows of my bedroom.*

*I sometimes see a monkey wandering the branches,
way out there, amidst the birds and the shadows.
He must have belonged to someone once. Maybe he
ran away, or his owner abandoned him. I feel for
him. Like me, he is a foreign body in this city.*

A foreign body.

*The children throw stones at him, the women drive
him off with sticks. They shout at him. Insult him.*

I've given him a name: Che Guevara, because he has a rather
rebellious look about him, a bit of a joker, and he is haughty
like a king who has lost his kingdom and his crown.

One time I found him out on the terrace eating bananas.
I don't know how he gets up there. Maybe by jumping from
the branches of the mulemba to one of the windows and from
there onto the ledge. It doesn't bother me. There are plenty of
bananas and pomegranates for us both – for now, at least.

I like opening up the pomegranates, turning their brightness
around in my fingers. I even like the Portuguese word
for them – romã – the morning glimmer it has to it.

THE SECOND LIFE OF
JEREMIAS CARRASCO

Any one of us, over the course of our lives, can know many different existences. Or occasionally, desistances. Not many, however, are given the opportunity to wear a different skin. But Jeremias Carrasco had something very like this happen to him. He awoke, after facing a careless firing squad, in a bed that was too short for his metre eighty-five, and so narrow that were he to uncross his arms they would both hang down, one on each side, with fingers touching the cement floor. He had a lot of pain in his mouth, neck and chest, and terrible trouble breathing. He saw, on opening his eyes, a low ceiling that was discoloured and cracked. A small gecko, hanging directly above him, was studying him curiously. The morning was making its way in, sinuous and scented, through a tiny window high up on the facing wall, just below the ceiling.

I've died, thought Jeremias. I've died, and that gecko is God.

Even supposing that the gecko was indeed God, He would appear to be hesitating about what fate to assign him. To Jeremias, this indecision was even stranger than finding himself face to face with the Creator, and the fact that He had taken on the form of a reptile. Jeremias knew, and had known for quite some time, that he was destined to burn for all eternity in the flames of Hell. He had killed, he had tortured. And if he'd started off doing those things out of duty, obeying orders, he had later acquired a taste for it. He only felt awake, whole, when he was racing through the night in pursuit of other men.

'Make your mind up,' said Jeremias to the gecko. Or rather, tried to say, but all that came out of his mouth was a dull tangled thread of sounds. He made a second attempt and, as in a nightmare, the dark rush of noise came again.

'Don't try and talk. Actually, you're not going to talk ever again.'

Jeremias believed, for some moments, that it was God who was condemning him to eternal silence. Then he turned his eyes to the right and saw a hugely fat woman leaning against the door. Her hands, with their tiny, fragile fingers, danced before her as she spoke:

'Yesterday they announced your death in the newspapers. They published a photograph – it was quite an old one, I almost didn't recognise you. They said you were a devil. You died, you were reborn and you have another chance. Make the most of it.'

Madalena had been working at the Maria Pia hospital for five years. Before that she had been a nun. A neighbour had witnessed the shooting of the mercenaries at a distance and had notified her. The nurse drove to the site on her own. One of the men was still alive. A bullet had passed through his chest, on a miraculous, perfect course that hadn't hit a single vital organ. A second projectile had gone into his mouth, shattering his two upper incisors, then perforating his throat.

'I don't understand what happened. Were you trying to catch the bullet in your teeth?' She laughed, her body shaking. The light seemed to laugh with her. 'Yes sir, those are some good reflexes. And it wasn't even such a bad idea, either. If the bullet hadn't found your teeth, it would have taken a different direction. It would have killed you or left you paralysed. I thought it best not to take you to hospital. They would take care of you and then, when you were recovered, they'd only shoot you again. So be patient, and I'll look after you myself with what little resources there are. I just have to get you out of Luanda. I don't know how long I'll be able to hide you. If the comrades find you, they'll shoot me too. As soon as possible we'll travel south.'

She hid him for nearly five months. By listening to the radio, Jeremias was able to follow the difficult progress of the government troops, supported by the Cubans, against the improvised, unstable alliance between the UNITA party, the National Front, the South African army, and mercenaries from Portugal, England and North America.

Jeremias was dancing on the beach in Cascais with a platinum blonde, and he had never been in a war, never killed, never tortured anyone, when Madalena shook him:

'Come on, captain! We go today or never.'

The mercenary sat up in bed, with some effort. The rain was crackling in the darkness, muffling the noise of what sparse traffic there was at that time. They were to travel in a little old van, a Citroën 2CV, its yellow bodywork badly worn, partly eaten away by rust, but with its engine in perfect working order. Jeremias stretched out on the back seat, hidden by various crates of books.

'Books instil respect,' explained the nurse. 'If you carry crates full of beer bottles, the soldiers will search every inch of the vehicle. Besides which, you'd get to Moçâmedes without a single bottle left.'

Her strategy proved correct. At the many checkpoints they passed through, the soldiers stood to attention when they saw the books, many apologising to Madalena, and let her go on her way. They arrived in Moçâmedes on an airless morning. Jeremias saw, through a small hole in the rusty side of the vehicle, a little town, dazed and spinning slowly about itself like a drunk at a funeral. Months earlier, the South African troops had come through here on their way to Luanda, easily crushing a troop made up of *pioneiros* and Mucubals.

Madalena parked the van in front of a solid blue mansion. She got out, leaving Jeremias to bake inside. The mercenary was sweating heavily. He could barely breathe. It would be preferable to get out too, he thought, even if it meant risking arrest, getting himself killed. He couldn't push the crates aside. He started kicking at the metal. An old man came over:

'Who's in there?'

Then he heard Madalena's gentle voice:

'I'm taking a little goat over to Virei.'

'But Virei's full of goats already! Ha ha! Imagine taking a goat to Virei!'

When the van was moving again, a bit of fresh air began to come in. Jeremias settled down. They drove for more than an hour, bumping about along secret routes through a landscape that seemed, to Jeremias, to be made entirely of hard winds, stone, dust and barbed wire. Finally, they stopped. A commotion of voices surrounded the vehicle. The back door opened and someone pulled out the boxes. There were dozens of curious faces. Women with their bodies painted red. Some of them quite old. Others still adolescent, their breasts pert and nipples swollen. Tall lads who looked very elegant indeed, each with a tuft of hair on the top of his head.

'My late father was born in the desert. He was buried here. These people are very devoted to him,' explained Madalena. 'They'll take you in and hide you for as long as necessary.'

The mercenary sat down on the floor, straightened his shoulders like a king parading naked, his silhouette the prickly shadow of a mutiati tree. A group of children surrounded him, touched him, pulled his hair. The young men laughed loudly. They were fascinated by the rough silence of this man, his distant gaze, the spectre of a past they sensed was violent and troubled. Madalena said goodbye with a slight nod:

'Wait here. They'll come for you. When everything calms down you'll be able to cross the border to South-West Africa. I imagine you have good friends among the white men.'

Years passed. Decades. Jeremias never crossed the border.

MAY 27TH

MAY 27TH

Che Guevara was very agitated this morning.

He was jumping from branch to branch. Crying out.

Later, looking out of the living room window,
I saw a man, running.

A tall fellow, really thin, incredibly agile. Three soldiers
were running after him, close behind. Throngs of people were
streaming from the corners, in bursts, joining the soldiers.
Within moments there was a whole crowd in pursuit of the
fugitive. I saw him crash into a boy who was crossing in
front of him on a bicycle, and he tumbled, flailing, into the
dust. The mob was about to reach him, it was just an arm's
length from him, when the man jumped onto the bicycle
and resumed his flight. By now a second group had formed,
a hundred metres further along the road, and there were
stones raining down. The poor wretch ducked into a narrow
alleyway. If he could have seen a bird's-eye view, like I could,

he never would have done it. A dead end. When he realised
his mistake, he ditched the bike and tried to jump the wall.

A tossed stone hit the back of his neck and he fell.

The throng reached him. They launched themselves, kicking,
onto his thin body. One of the soldiers drew a pistol and fired
it into the air, clearing a way through. He helped the man to
his feet, holding the pistol pointed towards the crowd. The
other two were shouting orders, attempting to calm tempers.
Finally they managed to make the crowd move back, they
dragged the prisoner off to a van, threw him inside and left.

I haven't had electricity for over a week. So I haven't listened
to the radio. I have no way of knowing what's going on.

I was woken by gunshots. Later, looking through the
living room window, I saw the really thin man, running.
Phantom roamed about all day, going round and round
his own fear, gnawing on his toes. I heard shouts in the
next-door apartment. Several men arguing. Then, silence.

I couldn't sleep. At four in the morning
I went up onto the terrace.

The night, like a well, was swallowing stars.

Then I saw a flatbed truck go by, laden with dead bodies.

ON THE SLIPPAGES OF REASON

Monte didn't like interrogations. For years he avoided discussing the subject. He'd even avoided recalling the seventies, when in order to preserve the socialist revolution, certain excesses – to use a euphemism for which we're indebted to the agents of the political police – were permitted. He confessed to his friends that he learned a lot about human nature while he was interrogating fractionists, and young men linked to the far left, in the terrible years that followed Independence. People with a happy childhood, he said, tend to be hard to break.

Perhaps he was thinking of Little Chief.

Little Chief – who had been baptised Arnaldo Cruz – didn't like talking about the periods he'd spent in detention. Orphaned at an early age, raised by his paternal grandmother, old Dulcineia, a professional sweet-seller, he'd wanted for nothing. He completed high school, and then, when everyone expected him to go to university and become a doctor, he became involved in political gatherings and got himself locked up. He had been imprisoned in Campo de São Nicolau, a little over a hundred kilometres from Moçâmedes, for four months when the Carnation Revolution broke out in Portugal. He reappeared in Luanda as a hero. Old Dulcineia believed her grandson would be made a minister, but Little Chief had more enthusiasm than actual talent for the intrigues of politics, and just a few months after Independence, by which time he was a law student, he was locked up again. His grandmother could not bear the grief. She died from a heart attack, days later.

Little Chief managed to escape from prison, hiding inside a coffin, a burlesque episode that deserves a lengthier account at a later point. Once out, he disappeared into anonymity. And yet, instead of taking refuge in a dark room somewhere, or even inside a wardrobe in the house of an elderly aunt, like some of his friends did, he chose the opposite solution. It's easiest to hide in plain sight, he thought. And so he wandered the streets, ragged, his hair in long tangled locks, covered in mud and tar. To make himself disappear still further, to escape the raids of the soldiers who moved about the city day and night, rounding up cannon fodder, he pretended to be crazy. But a person can only pass for insane, they can only make people believe this, if they really do go a bit crazy in the process.

'Imagine falling half asleep,' explained Little Chief. 'Part of you is alert, the other rambles. The part that rambles is the public part.'

It was in this state of social near-invisibility and semi-dementia, his lucidity travelling like a stowaway, that Little Chief saw the pigeon:

'Days of hunger. I could barely stand, the slightest breeze would have carried me off. I constructed a slingshot, with a stick and a few strips of rubber, and I was trying to hunt down some rats over in Catambor when a pigeon came down, all aglow, its whiteness lightening everything around it. I thought: it's the Holy Ghost. I looked for a stone, fixed my eye on the pigeon, and fired. A perfect shot. It was dead before it hit the ground. I immediately noticed the small plastic cylinder attached to a ring. I opened it, took out the little slip of paper, and read: *Tomorrow. Six o'clock, usual place. Be very careful. I love you.* It was when I gutted the pigeon to grill it that I found the diamonds.'

Little Chief didn't understand right away what had happened:

'In my failure to understand, I thought it was God giving me the stones. I even thought it was God who'd written me the message. My usual place was in front of the Lello bookshop. The next day, at six o'clock, there I was, waiting for God to show himself.'

God showed himself, in mysterious ways, via a hugely fat woman with a smooth, shining face and an expression of permanent delight. The woman got out of a small van, an old Citroën 2CV, and approached Little Chief, who was watching her, half hidden behind a dumpster.

'Hey, handsome!' cried Madalena. 'I need your help.'

Little Chief walked over to her, alarmed. The woman said she'd often watched him. It annoyed her to see a man in perfect condition, actually in *truly* perfect condition, spending his day sprawled out on the street playing the madman. The ex-con straightened himself up, unable to hold back his indignation:

'But I am extremely crazy, actually—'

'Not crazy enough,' the nurse cut him short. 'A real crazy person would try to appear a bit more circumspect.'

Madalena had inherited a small farm close to Viana that produced fruit and vegetables, which were so hard to find in the capital, and she was looking for someone who could keep an eye on the property. Little Chief accepted. Not for the obvious reasons, that he was broken with hunger and on a farm he'd get to eat every day. That he'd be safe from the soldiers, the police and other predators. He accepted because he believed it was the will of God.

Five months later, well fed, even better slept, he had fully recovered his lucidity. In his case, unfortunately, lucidity proved itself an enemy of good sense. He would have been better off staying insane for five or six more years. Thinking clearly now, his uneasiness returned. The country's collapse pained him in his soul, as if this were an actual organ with blood flowing through it. The pain was all the greater because of the fate of the companions he had left behind bars. Gradually, he reformed old connections. Together with a young footballer, Maciel Lucamba, whom he had met in Campo de São Nicolau, he constructed an imaginative plan that would entail the rescuing of a group of prisoners, and their escape on a trawler to Portugal. He never spoke to anyone of the diamonds. Not even to Maciel. He meant to sell the stones in order to pay for part of the operation. He didn't know to whom he might sell them, and he wasn't allowed the time to give this any thought. One Sunday afternoon, while he was resting, stretched out on a mat, two guys burst in suddenly and he was arrested. It pained him to learn that Madalena had been detained, too.

66

Monte interrogated him. He was hoping to demonstrate the nurse's involvement in the conspiracy. He promised to free them both if the young man revealed the whereabouts of a Portuguese mercenary whom Madalena had saved. Little Chief could have told the truth, that he had never heard of this mercenary. He thought, however, that exchanging even a handful of words with the agent would be tantamount to acknowledging his legitimacy, and so he merely spat on the floor. The stubbornness left him with scars on his body.

For the whole time he was detained, he kept the diamonds with him. Neither the guards nor the other prisoners ever suspected that this humble young man, always so concerned about other people, could be hiding a small fortune. On the morning of 27 May 1977, he was woken by a fierce din. Gunshots. A man he didn't recognise opened the door to his cell and shouted that he could leave if he wanted. A group in revolt had occupied the prison. The young man made his way through the commotion, calm as a ghost, feeling much more non-existent than when he used to roam the streets disguised as a madman. In the yard, sitting in the shade of a frangipani, he found a highly respected poetess, a historic name from the nationalist movement who, like him, had been detained just a few days after Independence, accused of supporting a strand of intellectuals who had been criticising the party leadership. Little Chief asked after Madalena. She had been released weeks earlier. The police had been unable to prove a thing against her. 'Amazing woman!' added the poetess. She advised Little Chief not to leave the prison. In her opinion, the revolt would be quickly stifled and the fugitives taken, tortured and shot:

'There's a bloodbath on the way.'

He agreed. He held her tight in a long hug, then went, dazed, into the torrential light of the streets. He considered looking for Madalena. He wanted to offer her his most profuse apologies. But he knew that this might cause her even more problems. Her house would be the first place the police would look for him. So he wandered the city, dazed, distressed, now following – at a distance – the groups of protestors, now accompanying the movements of the forces loyal to the president. He was walking this way and that, ever more lost, when a soldier recognised him. The man started to chase after him, crying 'Fractionist! Fractionist!' and within moments a crowd had assembled to run him down. Little Chief was a metre eighty-five tall, with long legs. During his adolescence he had been an athlete. The months he'd spent in a narrow cell, however, had made him shorter of breath. For the first five hundred metres he managed to get some distance between himself and his pursuers. He even believed that he would shake them off. Unfortunately, the commotion attracted yet more people. He felt his chest bursting. Sweat was running into his eyes, clouding his sight. A bicycle sprung out, suddenly, in front of him. He wasn't able to dodge past and fell on top of it. He got up, grabbed hold of it and once more managed to gain some distance. He veered right. A dead end. He left the bicycle and tried to jump the wall. A stone hit him on the back of the neck. He felt the taste of blood in his mouth, dizziness. The next moment he was in a car, handcuffed, a soldier on each side, and everybody shouting.

'You're going to die, reptile!' yelled the one who was driving.

'We've got orders to kill you all. But first I'm going to pull out your nails, one by one, till you tell us everything you know. I want those fractionists' names.'

He didn't pull out any of his nails at all. A lorry crashed into them at the next junction, throwing the car against the pavement. The door furthest from the collision opened, and Little Chief was spat out along with one of the soldiers. With some difficulty he got up, scattering blood, his own and others', and shards of glass. He didn't even have time to understand what was happening. A stocky guy with a smile that seemed to gleam with sixty-four teeth approached him, put a coat over him to hide the handcuffs, and dragged him away. Fifteen minutes later, the two of them went into a building that was elegant, albeit rather dilapidated. They climbed eleven floors on foot, Little Chief limping badly, as his right leg had nearly been broken.

The elevators weren't working, the man with the brilliant smile apologised:

'These hicks toss their rubbish into the elevator shaft. There's rubbish almost all the way up.'

He invited him in. On the living room wall, which was painted a shocking pink, there was a very conspicuous oil painting depicting, with naïve brushstrokes, the happy owner. There were two women sitting on the floor beside a small, battery-powered radio. One of them, who was very young, was breastfeeding a baby. Neither paid him any notice. The man with the brilliant smile pulled over a chair. He gestured to Little Chief to sit down. He took a paperclip from his pocket and straightened it out, then he leaned over the handcuffs, inserted the wire into the lock, counted to three, and opened it. He shouted something in Lingala. The older woman got up, without a word, and disappeared into the apartment. She returned, some minutes later, with two bottles of Cuca beer. An irate voice was yelling on the radio:

We must find them, tie them up and shoot them!

The man with the brilliant smile shook his head:

'This wasn't what we made our Independence for. Not for Angolans to kill one another like rabid dogs.' He sighed. 'Now we must treat your injuries. Then, rest. We have an extra room. You will stay there till the chaos is over.'

'It could take quite some time for the chaos to be over.'

'But end it will, comrade. Even evil needs to take a rest sometimes.'

THE REBEL AERIAL

In the first months of her isolation, Ludo only rarely went without the security of her umbrella when she visited the terrace. Later, she began using a long cardboard box, in which she had cut two holes at eye level for looking through, and two others to the sides, lower down, to keep her arms free. Thus equipped, she could work on the flowerbeds, planting, picking, weeding. From time to time she would lean out over the terrace wall, bitterly studying the submerged city. Anybody looking at the building from another of a similar height would see a large box moving around, leaning out and drawing itself back in again.

Clouds surrounded the city, like jellyfish.

They reminded Ludo of jellyfish.

When people look at clouds they do not see their real shape, which is no shape at all, or maybe every shape, because they are constantly changing. They see whatever it is that their heart yearns for.

You don't like that word – 'heart'?

Very well, choose another, then: soul, unconscious, fantasy, whatever you think best. None of them will be quite the right word.

Ludo watched the clouds and she saw jellyfish.

She had got into the habit of talking to herself, saying the same words over and over for hours on end: Chirping. Flocking. Twittering. Hovering. Flight. Chirping. Flocking. Twittering. Hovering. Flight. Chirping. Flocking. Twittering. Hovering. Flight. Chirping. Flocking. Twittering. Hovering. Flight. Chirping. Flocking. Twittering. Hovering. Flight. Good words, which dissolved like chocolate on the roof of her mouth and brought happy memories to mind. She believed that as she said them, as she evoked them, birds would return to the skies of Luanda. It had been years since she'd seen pigeons, seagulls. Not so much as one lost little bird. Night-time brought bats. The flight of bats, however, has nothing to do with the flight of birds. Bats, like jellyfish, are beings of no substance. See a bat streaking across the shadows and you don't think of it as a thing of flesh, of blood, of concrete bones and heat and sensations. Elusive shapes, quick ghosts amid the ruins, they're there, now they're gone. Ludo hated bats. Dogs were rarer than pigeons, and cats rarer than dogs. The cats were the first to disappear. The dogs held out on the city streets for some years. Wild packs of pedigree dogs. Gangly greyhounds, heavy asthmatic mastiffs, demented Dalmatians, disappointed pointers, and then, for another two or three years, the unlikely and despicable mixing of these many and once-so-noble pedigrees.

Ludo sighed. She sat down facing the window. From there she could see only the sky. Low, dark clouds, and remnants of a blue almost completely defeated by the darkness.

She remembered Che Guevara. She had grown used to seeing him, gliding along the walls, running across patios and roof-tops, seeking refuge in the highest branches of the enormous mulemba tree. It had done her good to see him. They were closely related beings, both of them mistakes, foreign bodies in the exultant organism of this city. People had thrown stones at the monkey. Others would throw poisoned fruit. The animal avoided it. He would sniff at the fruit and then move away with an expression of disgust. Shifting position slightly, Ludo could look at the satellite dishes. Dozens, hundreds, thousands of them, covering the rooftops of the buildings like a fungus. For a long time she had seen all of them turned towards the north. All of them, except one – the rebel aerial. Another mistake. She used to think she wouldn't die as long as that aerial kept its back to its companions. As long as Che Guevara survived, she wouldn't die. It had been more than two weeks, however, since she'd last seen the monkey, and in the early hours of that morning, as she first glanced out over the rooftops, she saw the aerial turned northward – like the others. A darkness, thick and burbling, like a river, spilled down over the windowpanes. Suddenly a great flash lit everything up, and the woman saw her own shadow thrown against the wall. The thunderclap rever-berated a second later. She shut her eyes. If she died here, like this, in a lucid moment, while out there the sky was dancing, triumphant and free, that would be good. Decades would go by before anyone found her. She thought about Aveiro, and realised that she had stopped feeling Portuguese. She didn't belong to anywhere. Over there, where she had been born, it was cold. She could see them again, the narrow streets, people walking, heads down against the wind and their own weariness. Nobody was waiting for her.

She knew, even before opening her eyes, that the storm was moving off. The sky was clearing. A ray of sunlight warmed her face. From up on the terrace she heard a whine, a weak complaint. Phantom, stretched out at her feet, leapt up, ran across the apartment to the living room, ran up the spiral staircase, tripping over himself, and disappeared. Ludo raced after him. The dog had cornered the monkey against the banana tree, and he was growling, nervous, head down. Ludo grabbed him by the collar, firmly, pulling him towards her. The German Shepherd resisted. He made as if to bite her. The woman smacked him on the nose with her left hand, again and again. Finally, Phantom gave in. He let himself be dragged away. She tied him up in the kitchen, shut the door and returned to the terrace. Che Guevara was still there, watching her with light, wondering eyes. She had never even seen such an intensely human look in the eyes of any man. On his right leg she could see a gash that was deep and clean, that looked like it had been made just moments earlier by a machete blow. The blood was mixing with rainwater.

Ludo peeled a banana, which she had brought from the kitchen, and held her arm out. The monkey leaned forward, sticking out his muzzle. He shook his head, in a gesture that might have indicated pain, or distrust. The woman called sweetly to him:

'Come on now, come on little one. Come, I'll look after you.'

The animal approached, dragging his leg, crying sadly.

Ludo let go of the banana and grabbed him by the neck. With her left hand she drew the knife she had at her waist and buried it in the lean flesh. Che Guevara gave a cry, broke free, the blade stuck in his belly, and with two big jumps he reached the wall. He stopped there, leaning against the wall, wailing, spattering blood. The woman sat down on the floor, exhausted. She, too, was crying. They stayed like that a long while, the two of them, looking at each other, until it started raining again. Then Ludo got up, walked over to the monkey, pulled out the knife and slit his throat.

In the morning, as she salted the meat, Ludo noticed that the rebel aerial was once again turned towards the south.

That aerial, and three others.

THE DAYS SLIDE BY AS IF
THEY WERE LIQUID

The days slide by as if they were liquid. I have no more notebooks to write in. I have no more pens either. I write on the walls, with pieces of charcoal, brief lines.

I save on food, on water, on fire and on adjectives.

I think about Orlando. I hated him, at first. Then I began to see his appeal. He could be very seductive. One man and two women under the same roof – a dangerous combination.

HAIKAI

I am oyster-sized
kept apart here with my pearls

.

.

.

shards in the abyss

THE SUBTLE ARCHITECTURE OF CHANCE

The man with the brilliant smile was called Bienvenue Ambrosio Fortunato. Not many people knew him by that name. At the end of the sixties he'd composed a bolero entitled 'Papy Bolingô'. The song, which was performed by François Luambo Luanzo Makiadi, the great Franco, had been an immediate hit, played day and night on the radios of Kinshasa, and the young guitar player earned himself a nickname that would accompany him for the rest of his life. A little over twenty years old, persecuted by the regime of Joseph-Désiré Mobutu, a.k.a. Mobutu Sese Seko Kuku Ngbendu waza Banga, Papy Bolingô had sought exile in Paris. He first got work as a doorman at a nightclub, and later as a guitarist in a circus band. It was in France that he made contact with the small Angolan community and redis-covered the country of his ancestors. As soon as Angola became independent, he packed his bags and set off for Luanda. He performed at weddings and other private parties frequented by Angolans who had returned from Zaire, and by true Zaireans pining for their homeland. The daily bread, which was so hard to earn, he managed to get through his work as a sound technician at Rádio Nacional. He was on duty the morning of 27 May, when the rebels entered the building. He then witnessed the arrival of the Cuban soldiers, who quickly put the house in order with slaps and kicks, retaking control of the broadcast.

As he left, very disturbed by the events he had witnessed, he saw a military truck ploughing into a car. He ran over to save the occupants. He immediately recognised one of the wounded men, a chubby guy with short, strong arms, who had on one occasion questioned him at the radio station. Then he noticed the tall young man, gaunt as an Egyptian mummy, his wrists cuffed together. He didn't hesitate. He helped the young man to his feet, covered his hands with his jacket, and brought him to his apartment.

'Why did you help me?'

Little Chief asked this question over and over, countless times, during the four years he spent hidden in the sound technician's apartment. His friend rarely answered. He gave a big laugh, the laugh of a free man, shook his head, changed the subject. One day he looked him straight in the eye:

'My father was a priest. He was a good priest and an excellent father. To this day I don't trust priests without children. How can you be a priest, if you aren't a father? Mine taught us to help the weak. And that time, when I saw you sprawled out on the pavement, you sure looked pretty weak to me. Besides, I recognised one of policemen, a security officer, who had been at my work interrogating people. I don't like the thought police. I never have. So I did what my conscience told me.'

Little Chief spent long months hidden away. After the death of the first president, the regime experimented with a hesitant opening-up. Those political prisoners not linked to the armed opposition were released. Some received invitations to occupy positions in the apparatus of the State. As he went out onto the streets of the capital, feeling somewhere between alarmed and intrigued, Little Chief discovered that almost everybody believed him dead. Some friends assured him they had actually been at his funeral. A few of his comrades in the struggle even seemed a little disappointed to be reunited with him quite so alive. As for Madalena, she received him joyfully. In the years that had passed she had set up an NGO, Stone Soup, committed to improving the diet of the communities living in Luanda's slum housing. She would go through the poorest neighbourhoods of the city, teaching the mothers and feeding the children, as best she could with the limited resources available.

'You can eat better without spending more,' she explained to Little Chief. 'You and your friends fill your mouths with big words – Social Justice, Freedom, Revolution – and meanwhile people waste away, they fall ill, many of them die. Speeches don't feed people. What the people need are fresh vegetables, and a good fish broth at least once a week. I'm only interested in the kinds of revolution that start off by getting people sat at the table.'

The young man was enthused by this. He started accompanying the nurse, in exchange for a symbolic wage – three meals a day, a bed and laundry. In the meantime, the years went by. The socialist system was dismantled by the very same people who had set it up, and capitalism rose from the ashes, as fierce as ever. Guys who just months ago had been railing against bourgeois democracy, at family lunches and parties, at demonstrations, in newspaper articles, were now dressed in designer clothing, driving around the city in cars that gleamed.

Little Chief allowed a thick prophet's beard to stretch down over his thin chest. He was still incredibly elegant and, despite the beard, retained a youthful look about him. However, he began to walk stooped slightly to the left, as though he were being pushed, from within, by a violent gale. One afternoon, seeing the rich people's cars parading past, he remembered the diamonds. Following Papy Bolingô's advice, he went over to the Roque Santeiro market. He was carrying a piece of paper with a name on it. He thought, as he allowed himself to be dragged along by the crowd, that it would be impossible to track anyone down in the vastness of that chaos. He was afraid he would never be able to get out. He was wrong. The first trader he approached pointed him in one particular direction. Another, a few metres on, confirmed it. After fifteen minutes he stopped outside a shack on whose door someone had painted, in rough strokes, the torso of a woman, with a long neck, lit up by a diamond necklace. He knocked. He was met by a slim man in a pink jacket and trousers and a livid-red tie and hat. His shoes, which were highly polished, shone in the gloom. Little Chief remembered the *sapeurs* Papy Bolingô had introduced him to, years earlier, on a short visit to Kinshasa. '*Sapeurs*' are what they call the fashion-mad in the Congo. Guys who dress in clothes that are expensive and showy, spending everything they have, and some that they don't have, to walk the streets like models on a catwalk.

He went inside. He saw a desk and two chairs. A rotating fan attached to the ceiling was disturbing the drenched air with slow strokes.

'Jaime Panguila,' the *sapeur* introduced himself, gesturing for him to sit.

Panguila was interested in the stones. First, he examined them by the light of an oil lamp. Then he took them to the window, drew open the curtain, and studied them, turning them around between his fingers under the harsh rays of a sun almost at its peak. Finally, he sat down:

'These stones, though small, are good, very pure. I don't want to know how you got hold of them. I'd be risking a lot of trouble by trying to put them on the market. I can't offer you more than seven thousand dollars.'

He refused. Panguila doubled the offer. He drew a wad of notes from one of the desk drawers, put it into a shoebox and pushed it towards the other man.

Little Chief went to sit in a nearby bar, with the shoebox on top of the table, to think about what he was going to do with the money. He noticed the logo on his beer bottle, the silhouette of a bird with wings spread, and he remembered the pigeon. He had kept the paper in the plastic tube, on which it was still possible to read, albeit with some difficulty:

Tomorrow. Six o'clock, usual place. Be very careful. I love you.

Who might have written that?

Perhaps a senior official at the Diamang mining company. He imagined a man with a severe expression, scribbling out the message, putting the note into the plastic cylinder and then attaching it to the leg of the pigeon. He imagined him putting the diamonds into the bird's beak, first one and then the other, and then releasing it, and it flying off from a residence that was sunk amid tall, leafy mango trees into Dundo, to the perilous skies of the capital. He imagined it flying above the dark forests, the astonished rivers, the many armies pitted in conflict.

He got up, smiling. He already knew what to do with the money. In the months that followed he devised and established a small delivery service, which he named Pigeon-Post. The Portuguese word for pigeon also meant 'messenger' in Kimbundo, and the coincidence pleased him. The company prospered, and new projects came along to join it. He invested in several different areas, from hotels to real estate, always successfully.

One Sunday afternoon, it was December and the air was dazzlingly bright, he met Papy Bolingô at Rialto. They ordered some beers. They chatted without any urgency, slow and chilled, stretching out into the langour of the afternoon as if in a hammock.

'And life, Papy?'

'Goes on living.'

'And what about you, still singing?'

'Not very much, bro. I haven't been doing the act. Fofo has been a bit funny lately.'

Papy Bolingô had been sacked from Rádio Nacional. He'd been surviving, with great effort, by playing at parties. One of his cousins, a hunting-party guide, had brought him a pygmy hippo from the Congo. The guide had found the animal in the forest when it was still a baby, desperately watching over its mother's dead body. The guitar player had brought the animal to his apartment. He fed it from a baby's bottle. He taught it to dance the Zaire rumba. Fofo, the hippo, started to join him when he performed at small bars on the outskirts of Luanda. Little Chief had seen the show several times, and he'd always come out feeling impressed. The problem was that the hippo had grown too much. Pygmy hippos, or dwarf hippos (*Choeropsis liberiensis*) may look small compared to their better-known relatives, but by the time they are adults they can grow to the volume of a large pig. The protests from the neighbours in the building grew. Many of them owned dogs. Some insisted on raising chickens on their verandas, or goats, occasionally pigs. No one had hippos. A hippopotamus, even if this particular one was an artist, frightened the residents. Some of them, when they saw him out on the veranda, threw stones.

Little Chief saw that the time had come to help his friend.

'How much do you want for your place? I need a good apartment, right in the heart of the capital. You need a farm, a big open space, to raise the hippo.'

Papy Bolingô hesitated.

'I've been in that apartment so many years now, I think I've become attached to it.'

'Five hundred thousand?'

'Five hundred thousand? Five hundred thousand what?'

'I'll give you five hundred thousand dollars for the apartment. You can buy yourself a nice farm with money like that.'

Papy Bolingô laughed, amused. Then he noticed the seriousness of his friend's face and his laughter stopped. He straightened up:

'I thought you were kidding. You've got five hundred thousand dollars?'

'And several million more. Many million. I'm not doing you a favour, I think it's an excellent investment. Your building is pretty shabby, but with a good coat of paint, and new elevators, it'll get its old colonial charm back. Before too long, buyers are going to start showing up. Generals. Ministers. People with a lot more money than me. They'll pay some paltry sums for people to leave. Those who don't leave nicely will be made to do it nastily.'

That was how Little Chief ended up with Papy Bolingô's apartment.

BLINDNESS

I've been losing my eyesight. I close my right eye and
I can only see shadows now. Everything confuses me.
I walk clinging on to the walls. It's a struggle to read, and
I can only do that in sunlight, using stronger and stronger
magnifying glasses. I reread my last remaining books, the
ones I refuse to burn. I have been burning the beautiful
voices that have kept me company over all these years.

I sometimes think: I've gone mad.

I saw, from out on the terrace, a hippopotamus dancing
on the veranda of the apartment next door. An illusion,
I'm quite aware of that, but I did see it just the same.
It might be hunger. I've been feeding myself very badly.

My weakness, my vanishing eyesight, it means I stumble over
letters as I read. I read pages I've read so many times before, but
they're different now. I get things wrong, as I read, and in those
mistakes, sometimes, I find incredible things that are right.

99

In these mistakes I find myself, often.

Some pages are improved by these mistakes.

A sparkle of fireflies, fireflying through the rooms.
I move about, like a medusa jellyfish, in this illuminated haze.
I sink into my own dreams. One might perhaps call this dying.

I was happy in this home, on those afternoons when the sun
came into the kitchen to pay me a visit. I would sit down at the
table. Phantom would come over and rest his head in my lap.

If I still had the space, the charcoal, and available walls,
I could compose a great work about forgetting:
a general theory of oblivion.

I realise I have transformed the entire apartment into
a huge book. After burning the library, after I have died,
all that remains will be my voice.

In this house all the walls have my mouth.

THE COLLECTOR OF DISAPPEARANCES

During the years 1997 and 1998 five airplanes, originating in Belarus, Russia, Moldavia and Ukraine, disappeared from Angola's skies with a total of twenty-three crew. On 25 May 2003, a Boeing 727 belonging to American Airlines went astray from Luanda airport and was never seen again. The thing hadn't flown for fourteen months.

Daniel Benchimol collected stories of disappearances in Angola. All kinds of disappearances, though he preferred those of the air. It's always more interesting being snatched away by the heavens, like Jesus Christ or his mother, than being swallowed up by the earth. People or objects who are literally swallowed by the earth, as seemed to have happened to the French writer Simon-Pierre Mulamba, are, however, very rare.

The journalist classified the disappearances on a scale from one to ten. The five planes that disappeared from the skies above Angola, for example, were categorised by Benchimol as grade-eight disappearances. The Boeing 727, a grade-nine disappearance; Simon-Pierre Mulamba too.

Mulamba disembarked in Luanda on 20 April 2003, at the

invitation of the Alliance Française, for a conference on the life and work of Léopold Sédar Senghor. Tall, distinguished-looking, never without his beautiful felt hat, which he wore tilted just slightly to the right with studied indifference. Simon-Pierre liked Luanda. It was the first time he'd visited Africa. His father, a teacher of Latin dance, native of Ponta Negra, had told him about the heat, the humidity, warned him of the dangers of the women, but hadn't prepared him for this excess of life, for the merry-go-round of emotions, the intoxicating tumult of sounds and smells. On the second night, right after his lecture, the writer accepted an invitation from Elizabela Montez, a young architecture student, to have a drink at one of Ilha's smartest bars. The third night he spent dancing *mornas* and *coladeiras* in the backyard of some Cape Verdeans in Chicala, in the company of two of Elizabela's girlfriends. On the fourth night he disappeared. The French cultural attaché, who had arranged to meet him for lunch, went in search of him at the lodge where they had put him up, a really lovely place, close to the Barra do Kwanza. Nobody had seen him. There was no answer on his cell phone. In his room, the bedcovers had not yet been pulled back, the sheets still stretched tight, a chocolate on the pillow.

Daniel Benchimol learned of the writer's disappearance before the police. He only needed two telephone calls to discover, with a considerable amount of detail, where and with whom Simon-Pierre had spent his first nights. Two more calls and he knew that the Frenchman had been seen at five in the morning leaving a disco in the Quinaxixe market, a place frequented by European expats, slutty teenage girls, and poets with rather more interest in pursuing the booze than the muse. That night, Benchimol went to the disco himself. Fat, sweaty men were drinking in silence. Others, half hidden in the dark, stroked the bare knees of girls who were very young. He particularly noticed one of the girls because she was wearing a black felt hat with a thin red ribbon. He was about to approach her when a blond guy with his long hair tied into a ponytail gripped his arm:

'Queenie's with me.'

'Don't worry. I've just got a question I want to ask her,' Daniel reassured him.

'We don't like journalists. Are you a journalist?'

'Sometimes, pal, it depends. I mostly feel Jewish, though.'

The other man let go of him, confused. Daniel greeted Queenie:

'Good evening. I just wanted to know where you got the hat.'

The girl smiled:

'The French mulatto who was here yesterday, he lost it.'

'He lost the hat?'

'Or the other way round, he's the one who was lost. The hat found me.'

She explained that the previous night, a group of boys, those ones who live out on the street, had seen the Frenchman leave the club. He had stopped to urinate after a few metres, around the back of a building, and then the earth had swallowed him up. All that was left was the hat.

'The earth swallowed him up?'

'That's what they're saying, old man. It could be quicksand, it could be witchcraft, I don't know. The boys pulled the hat out with a stick. I bought the hat from them. It's mine now.'

Daniel left the disco. There were two boys watching television, sitting on the pavement in front of a shop window. The sound from the television didn't reach outside, so the two of them were improvising the dialogue for each of the actors in turn. The journalist had seen the film before. The new dialogue, however, had transformed the plot entirely. He spent a few minutes enjoying watching the show. He took advantage of a break to speak to the boys:

'I've heard there was a guy, a French guy, who disappeared near here last night. They say he was swallowed up by the earth.'

'Yes,' one of the children confirmed. 'These things happen.'

'Did you see it?'

'No. But Baiacu saw it.'

Daniel questioned other boys in the days that followed, and all spoke of Simon-Pierre's sad end as though they had witnessed it. Then, when pressed, they acknowledged that they had not been there. Certainly nobody saw the French writer again. The police filed the case.

There is only one grade-ten disappearance on the Benchimol Scale. The journalist witnessed that remarkable loss himself. On 28 April 1988 the *Jornal de Angola*, the newspaper for which Daniel was working, sent him to a small town called Nova Esperança, where twenty-five women had been murdered under suspicion of witchcraft. He was accompanied by a photographer, the famous Kota Kodak, or 'KK'. The two journalists disembarked from a commercial airliner at Huambo airport. There was a driver waiting to take them to

Nova Esperança. Once they were there, Daniel chatted to the chieftain and various members of the tribe. KK took their portraits. It was getting dark when they got back to Huambo. They were due to return to Nova Esperança the following morning, in an air-force helicopter. The pilot, however, proved unable to locate the village.

'It's weird,' he confessed, troubled, after two hours of wandering the skies. 'There's nothing at those coordinates. Nothing down there but grass.'

Daniel became impatient at the young man's ineptitude. He hired the same driver who'd first taken them there. KK refused to go with them:

'There's nothing to take pictures of. You can't photograph absences.'

They went round and round in the car, revisiting the same landscapes, as in a dream, for that infinite length of time that a dream can occupy, until the driver, too, admitted his embarrassment:

'We're lost!'

'We? You're the one who's lost!'

The man turned to face him in a rage, as though he thought him responsible for the lunacy of the world:

'These roads are more and more muddled.' He was pummelling the steering wheel hard. 'I think we've had a geographical accident!'

Suddenly, a bend loomed up in the road and they emerged from the mistake, or the illusion, dazed and trembling. They did not find Nova Esperança. A signpost did, however, return them to the highway, which in turn took them back to Huambo.

KK was waiting at the hotel, arms crossed across his thin chest, a dark expression on his face:

'Bad news, partner. I developed the film and it's all burned out. All the gear's complete crap. Gets worse every day.'

No one on the paper seemed concerned at the news that Nova Esperança had disappeared. The editor-in-chief, Marcelino Assumpção da Boa Morte, just laughed:

'The village disappeared? Everything's always disappearing in this country! Perhaps the whole country is in the process of disappearing, a village here, a village there. By the time we notice there'll be nothing left at all!'

In 2003, a few weeks after the mysterious disappearance of the French writer Simon-Pierre Mulamba, to which the Angolan newspapers gave a certain prominence, Marcelino Assumpção da Boa Morte called Daniel into his office. He held out a blue envelope:

'I've got something for you here, seeing as you collect disappearances. Read this. See if there might be a piece in it.'

THE LETTER

THE LETTER

Dear Managing Director of the Jornal de Angola,

My name is Maria da Piedade Lourenço Dias and I'm a clinical psychologist. About two years ago I discovered an awful truth: I was adopted. My biological mother handed me over for adoption immediately after my birth. I was confused, and decided to investigate why she did it. Ludovica Fernandes Mano – that is my biological mother's name – was brutally raped by a stranger in the summer of 1955, and became pregnant. Following this tragic event, she always lived in the house of an older sister, Odete, who in 1973 married a mining engineer, based in Luanda, called Orlando Pereira dos Santos.

They didn't come back to Portugal after Angola's Independence. The Portuguese consulate in Luanda has no record of any of them either. I'm presuming to write to you in order to find out whether your newspaper might in any way be able to help me find Ludovica Fernandes Mano.

Respectfully yours,
  Maria da Piedade Lourenço

THE DEATH OF PHANTOM

Phantom died in his sleep. In his last weeks he had been eating very little. To tell the truth, he had never eaten much – there wasn't much to eat – which perhaps explains how he had lived so long. Laboratory experiments show that the life expectancy of mice increases considerably when they are given a low-calorie diet.

Ludo woke up, and the dog was dead.

The woman sat down on the mattress, opposite the open window. She hugged her thin knees. She lifted her eyes towards the sky, where, bit by bit, pink, light clouds were forming. Chickens clucked on the terrace. The crying of a child rose up from the floor below. Ludo felt her chest emptying. Something – some dark substance – was escaping from inside her, like water out of a cracked vessel, slipping down onto the cold cement. She had lost the only creature in the world who loved her, and she had no tears to cry.

She stood up, chose a piece of charcoal, sharpened it, and attacked one of the walls, which was still clean, in the guest bedroom:

Phantom died tonight. Everything is so useless now.

The look in his eyes caressed me, explained me and sustained me.

She climbed up to the terrace without the protection of the old cardboard box. The day was unfurling itself, a warm yawn of a day. Maybe it was Sunday. The streets were almost deserted. She watched a group of women walk past dressed in pristine white. One of them, spotting her, raised her right hand in a joyful greeting.

Ludo drew back.

She could jump, she thought. Step forward. She could climb out onto the ledge, so simple.

The women, down there, would see her one moment – a feather-light shadow – hovering a second and then falling. She stepped back, went on stepping back, cornered by the blue, by the vastness, by the certainty that she would go on living, even with nothing to give life any meaning.

Death circles around me, shows its teeth, snarls. I kneel down and offer it my bare throat. Come, come, come now, friend. Bite. Let me go. Oh, you did come today and you forgot me. _ _ _ _ _ _ _ _ _ _ _ _ _ _ _ _ _ _ Night-time. It's night-time again. I've counted more nights than days. _ _ _ _ _ _ _ _ _ _ _ _ _ _ _ _ _ _ _ The nights, then, and the clamour of the frogs. I open the window and see the lagoon. The night that has split in two. _ _ _ _ _ _ _ _ _ _ _ _ _ _ _ _ _ _ _ It rains, everything overflows. At night, it's as though the darkness were singing. The night rising up in waves, devouring the buildings.

I think, once again, of that woman to whom I returned the pigeon. Tall, prominent bones, with that slight disdain with which very beautiful women make their way through reality. She walks through Rio de Janeiro, along the bank of Lagoa (I've seen photographs, I found several illustrated books about Brazil in the library). Cyclists pass her. The ones who let their gaze linger on her never come back. The woman is called Sara, I call her Sara.

She looks like she's out of a canvas by Modigliani.

ABOUT GOD AND OTHER TINY FOLLIES

I find it easier to have faith in God, notwithstanding His being something so far beyond our incredibly limited understanding, than in arrogant humanity. For many years, I called myself a believer out of sheer laziness. It would have been hard to explain my non-belief to Odete, to everyone else. I didn't believe in men either, but that was something people accepted easily. I have understood over these last years that in order to believe in God, it is essential to have trust in humanity. There is no God without humanity.

I continue not to believe – neither in God, nor in humanity. Since Phantom died I have worshipped His spirit. I talk to Him. I believe that He hears me. I believe this not through an effort of the imagination, still less intelligence, but by engaging another faculty entirely, which we might call unreason.

Am I talking to myself?

Perhaps. Just like the saints, by the way, who boasted
about talking to God. I'm less arrogant. I talk to myself,
believing that I'm talking to the sweet soul of a dog.
In any case, these conversations do me good.

EXORCISM

EXORCISM

I carve out verses
short
as prayers

words are
legions
of demons
expelled

I cut adverbs
pronouns

I spare my
wrists

THE DAY LUDO SAVED LUANDA

On the living room wall there hung a watercolour depicting a group of Mucubals dancing. Ludo had met the artist, Albano Neves e Sousa, a fun, playful kind of guy, an old friend of her brother-in-law's. She couldn't stand the picture at first. She saw in it a distillation of everything she hated about Angola: savages celebrating something – some cause of joy, some glad omen – that was quite alien to her. Then, bit by bit, over the long months of silence and solitude, she began to feel some affection towards those figures that moved, circling around a fire, as though life really deserved such elegance.

She burned the furniture, she burned thousands of books, she burned all the paintings. It wasn't until she was desperate that she took the Mucubals down off the wall. She was going to pull out the nail, just for aesthetic reasons, because it looked wrong there, serving no purpose, when it occurred to her that maybe this, this piece of metal, was holding up the wall. Maybe it was holding up the whole building. Who knows, if she pulled the nail out of the wall, the whole city might collapse.

She did not pull out the nail.

**APPARITIONS,
AND A NEARLY FATAL FALL**

November passed, cloudless. December too. February arrived and the air was cracked with thirst. Ludo saw the lagoon drying out. First it darkened, then the grass turned gold, almost white, and the night-time lost the uproarious noise of the frogs. The woman counted the bottles of water. Not many left. The chickens, which she gave the muddy water from the swimming pool to drink, fell sick. They all died. There was still corn left, and beans, but to cook them used up a lot of water, and she needed to save it.

She went hungry again. One morning she got up early, shaking off her nightmares, staggered into the kitchen, and saw a bread roll on the table:

'Bread!'

She picked it up in disbelief, with both hands.

She smelled it.

The scent of the bread carried her back to her childhood. She and her sister, on the beach, splitting some bread with butter. She bit into it. It was only when she had finished eating that she realised she was crying. She sat down, trembling.

Who could have brought her that bread?

Maybe someone had thrown it through the window. She imagined a broad-shouldered young man hurling a loaf of bread into the air. The bread tracing a slow arc, before landing on her table. The person in question might have thrown the bread up into the sky from the lagoon, which was now almost dry, as part of some mysterious ritual aimed at summoning the rain. A Quimbanda witch doctor, a real champion bread-thrower, since it was a quite considerable distance. That night she fell asleep early. She dreamed an angel had visited her.

In the morning she found, on the kitchen table, six bread rolls, a tin of guava jelly and a large bottle of Coca-Cola. Ludo sat down, her heart racing. Someone was coming in and out of her house. She got up. In recent months her eyesight had been getting worse and worse. No sooner had the light begun to fade, after a certain time of the day, than she began to move about just by instinct. She went up onto the terrace. She ran across to the building's right-hand façade, the only one without any windows, which faced another block just a few metres away. She leaned over and saw the scaffolding, which surrounded the neighbouring building, right up against her own. That was how the invader had come in. She went down the stairs. It might have been because of her nerves, or because of the lack of light, but whatever the reason, her instinct failed her, she missed a step and tumbled, flailing. She fainted. The moment she had recovered her senses she knew she had fractured her left femur. So that's how it's going to be, she thought. I'm going to die not the victim of some mysterious African affliction, not through lack of appetite or exhaustion, not murdered by a thief, not because the sky has fallen on my head, but conspired against by one of the most famous laws of physics: *Given two bodies of mass* m_1 *and* m_2, *and a distance* r *between them, these two bodies will be attracted to each other with a force proportional to the mass of each and inversely proportional to the square of the distance that separates them.* She had been saved by her lack of mass. Twenty kilos more and the impact would have been devastating. Pain climbed up her leg, paralysing the left side of her torso, preventing her from thinking clearly. She stayed immobile for quite some time, while night twisted about out there, like a boa constrictor, choking the harassed acacias on the streets and squares. The pain was barking, the pain was biting. Her mouth felt dry. She tried to spit out her tongue, because it was as though it didn't belong to her, a piece of cork trapped in her throat.

She thought about the bottle of Coca-Cola. About the bottles of water she kept in the pantry. She would need to drag herself fifteen metres or so. She stretched out her arms, braced her hands against the cement, straightened her trunk. It was as if her leg were being chopped off with the blade of an axe. She yelped. Her own yelp surprised her.

'I've woken the whole building,' she muttered.

She woke up Little Chief, in the next-door apartment. The businessman had been dreaming about the Kianda. He had been having the same dream for several nights. He would go out onto the veranda in the middle of the night and see a light gleaming in the lagoon. The light increased in volume, a rainbow that was round and musical, and in the meantime the businessman felt his body losing its weight. He awoke at the moment when the light rose to meet him. This time he woke earlier, because the light screamed, or it seemed to him as though the light was screaming, in a sudden explosion of mud and frogs. He sat up in bed, feeling stifled, his heart pounding. He remembered the time he had spent shut away in that same room. Sometimes he used to hear a dog barking. He'd hear the distant voice of a woman chanting old songs.

'The building is haunted,' Papy Bolingô had assured him. 'There's the barking dog, which no one's ever seen, like a kind of phantom dog. They say it can go through walls. You've got to be careful when you're asleep. The dog comes through the wall, it's barking, *bow-wow-wow*, but you don't see a thing, you just hear its barking, and then it inveigles itself into your dreams. You start having dreams that are really filled with barking. One of the residents, on the floor below, a young craftsman called Eustákio, woke up one morning and could no longer speak. He just barked. They took him to a traditional doctor, pretty well renowned, who took five days to remove the dog's spirit, and its barking, from Eustákio's head.'

Little Chief found the building's architecture peculiar. He was confused by the wall blocking off the corridor, an arrangement that didn't occur on the other floors. There had to be another apartment on that floor – but where was it?

Meanwhile, just a few metres away, on the other side of the wall, Ludo forced herself to move towards the kitchen. With each centimetre she felt further away from her own self. The first light of morning found her still in the living room, about two metres from the door. She was burning with fever.

Her thirst was troubling her more than the pain. Around two in the afternoon she reached the door. She fainted. She opened her eyes and saw, vaguely, a face before her. She brought her hands to her eyes, rubbed them. The face was still there. A boy, it looked to her like the face of a boy, with two big astonished eyes.

'Who are you?'

'My name's Sabalu.'

'Did you get in from the scaffolding?'

'Yes, I climbed the scaffolding. They put scaffolding on the building next door. They're painting it. The scaffolding comes nearly all the way up to your terrace. Then I piled some crates on the top level and climbed up. It was easy. What about you, did you fall?'

'How old are you?'

'Seven. Are you dying?'

'I don't know. I did start thinking I was dead already. Water. Go get me water.'

'Do you have money?'

'Yes, I'll give you all the money but go get me water.'

The boy got up. He glanced around him.

'There's hardly anything here. Not even furniture. Looks like you're poorer than me. Where've you got the money?'

'Water!'

'OK there, grandma, take it easy, I'll go fetch you a soda.'

He brought the bottle of Coca-Cola from the kitchen. Ludo drank straight from the bottle, greedily. She was struck by how sweet it was. It had been years since she'd felt the taste of sugar. She told the boy to go to the study to find her purse, where she kept the money. Sabalu came back, laughing hard as he scattered wads of banknotes around him.

'This isn't money any more, grandma, it's not worth anything.'

'There's silver cutlery. Take the silver cutlery.'

The boy laughed again.

'I've already taken them, didn't you even notice?'

'No. Was it you who brought the bread yesterday?'

'The day before. You don't want to call a doctor?'

'No, no, I don't!'

'I can call a neighbour. You must have neighbours.'

'No, no! Don't call anyone.'

'You don't like people? I don't like people either.'

Ludo started to cry.

'Go away. Go away.'

Sabalu got up.

'Where's the door to get out?'

'There isn't one. Leave the way you came.'

Sabalu put the rucksack on his back and disappeared. Ludo took a deep breath. She leaned on the wall. The pain was subsiding. Maybe she should have let the boy call a doctor. Then she thought that along with the doctor would come the police, then journalists, and she was keeping a skeleton on the terrace. She preferred to die here, a prisoner and yet free, just as she had lived the past thirty years.

Free?

Often, as she looked out over the crowds that clashed violently against the sides of the building, that vast uproar of car horns and whistles, cries and entreaties and curses, she experienced a profound terror, a feeling of siege and threat. Whenever she wanted to go out she would look for a book in the library. She felt, as she went on burning those books, after having burned all the furniture, the doors, the wooden floor tiles, that she was losing her freedom. It was as though she was incinerating the whole planet. When she burned Jorge Amado she stopped being able to visit Ilhéus and São Salvador. Burning *Ulysses*, by Joyce, she had lost Dublin. Getting rid of *Three Trapped Tigers*, she incinerated old Havana. There were fewer than a hundred books left. She kept them more out of stubbornness than to make any use of them. Her eyesight was so bad that even with an enormous magnifying glass, even holding the book in direct sunlight, sweating as though she were in a sauna, it took her an entire afternoon to decipher one page. In recent months, she had taken to writing her favourite lines from the books she had left in huge letters on those walls of the apartment that were still blank. It won't be long, she thought, and I really will be a prisoner. I don't want to live in a prison. She fell asleep. She was awoken by a quiet laugh. The boy was there again in front of her, a slender silhouette, cut out against the stormy glare of the sunset.

'Now what? You've already taken the cutlery. I don't have anything else.'

Sabalu laughed again.

'Tsh, grandma! I thought you'd died.'

He put his rucksack down at the lady's feet.

'I bought medicines. Loads of them. They'll help you.' He sat down on the floor. 'I also bought more Coke. And food, grilled chicken. You hungry?'

They ate just there, where they were, sharing the bread and the pieces of chicken. Sabalu showed her the medicines he had brought: painkillers, anti-inflammatories.

'I went to Roque Santeiro. I talked to this guy. I said my father had hit my mother, he broke her arm, and she's embarrassed to go to the doctor. Then he sold me all this. I paid with the money from the cutlery. There was loads left over. Can I sleep in your house?'

Sabalu helped the old lady up, took her to her room and lay her down on the mattress. Then he lay beside her and fell asleep. The next morning he went to the market and came back carrying vegetables, matches, salt, various spices and two kilos of beef. He also brought a portable stove, the kind for camping, with a small butane gas canister. He did the cooking himself, on the bedroom floor, following Ludo's instructions. They both ate with gusto. Then the boy did the washing-up and put away the crockery. He roamed about the house, curious:

'You know, you've got a lot of books.'

'A lot of books? Yes, I did have a lot. There aren't many now.'

'I've never seen so many.'

'Can you read?'

'I'm not very good at putting the letters together. I only did one year at school.'

'Would you like me to teach you? I'll teach you to read, and then you can read to me.'

Sabalu learned to read while Ludo convalesced. The old lady also taught him to play chess. The boy took to the board naturally. While he played he talked to her of his life out there.

For the woman it was like having an extra-terrestrial revealing the secrets of a distant planet to her. One afternoon, Sabalu discovered that the scaffolding was being taken down.

'How am I going to leave now?'

Ludo was fretting:

'I don't know!'

'Well, how did you come in?'

'I didn't come in. I've always lived in this house.'

The boy looked at her, confused. Ludo gave in. She took him to the front door. She opened it and showed him the wall she herself had put up, thirty years before, separating the apartment from the rest of the building.

'On the other side of this door is the world.'

'Can I break through the wall?'

'You can, but I'm afraid. I'm very afraid.'

'Don't be afraid, grandma. I'll protect you.'

The boy went to fetch a pickaxe, and with half a dozen violent blows opened a hole in the wall. Looking through it he saw, on the other side, the astonished face of Little Chief.

'Who are you?'

Sabalu widened the hole with two more blows. He introduced himself:

'My name's Sabalu Estevão Capitango, *senhor*. I'm busy breaking through this wall.'

The businessman shook the plaster dust off his jacket. He took two steps back:

'Jesus! What planet have you come from?'

The boy could have made use of the brilliant retort given by the singer Elza Soares at the start of her career, aged thirteen, scrawny, badly dressed, when Ary Barroso asked her the exact same question (behind him the audience was laughing at her. At home, her first child was dying): '*I've come from Planet Hunger.*' Sabalu, however, had never heard of Elza Soares, nor of Ary Barroso, so he shrugged and replied with a smile:

'We live here.'

'We?'

'Me and my grandmother.'

'You live there? There's an apartment on that side?'

'Sure is.'

'And you've been living there how long?'

'Always.'

'Oh really? And how do you get out?'

'We didn't go out. We just lived here. Now we will, though, we're going to start going out.'

Little Chief shook his head, stunned.

'Very well, very well. You finish breaking down that wall and then clean up the hallway. I don't want a speck of dust left, understand? This isn't a slum any more. It's a smart building now, well respected, like in the colonial days.'

He went back into his apartment, walked over to the kitchen, found a beer in the fridge. He went to drink it on the veranda. Sometimes he felt a kind of nostalgia for the days when, mad and wretched, he would spend his hours dancing out on the streets and the squares. The world, washed in sunlight, was not troubled by mysteries. Everything had seemed transparent to him then, and lucid – even God, who, assuming a variety of forms, so often appeared to him at evening-time for a couple of thimblefuls of pleasant conversation.

MUTIATI BLUES (1)

Today the Kuvale number no more than five thousand, but they occupy a vast area, more than half of Namibe Province. Nowadays they are a prosperous people, in terms of the things they value: they have copious head of oxen. With the exception of the northeast, their territories were spared almost any direct incidents in the war, there has been rain in recent years, at least enough to keep the cattle (there have even been some good years, and it has been a long time since there has been a really bad one), and yet the course Angola has taken puts them in a position of food poverty. They are unable to trade their oxen for corn. This apparent paradox – so many oxen yet so much hunger – is yet another way in which they are unusual. But isn't that true of Angola, too? So much oil...?

Ruy Duarte de Carvalho, 'Aviso à Navegação:
A brief introductory look at the Kuvale shepherds'

The detective squatted down. He fixed his gaze on the old man, who was sitting, very straight-backed, a few metres ahead of him. The brightness of the sky was dizzying, preventing him from seeing clearly. He turned to the guide:

'That old man over there, he's a mulatto?'

The guide smiled. The question seemed to unsettle him.

'Maybe. Some white man who came through here seventy years ago. These things happen. They still happen today. These guys offer their wives to the visitors, didn't you know that?'

'I'd heard.'

'They do it. But if the woman refuses, that's fine, they're under no obligation. Women have more power, here, than people think.'

'I don't doubt it. Here and everywhere else. Eventually women are going to end up with all the power.'

He addressed the old man:

'Do you speak Portuguese?'

The man he'd spoken to ran his right hand over his head, which was covered by a kind of hat, a really nice one, with red and yellow stripes. He looked straight at Monte in a silent challenge, opened his mouth – which was almost toothless – and gave the tiniest little laugh, a soft laugh that dispersed like dust into the luminous air. A lad who was sitting beside him made some comment to the guide. The guide translated it:

'He's saying the old man doesn't talk. Never has.'

Monte got up. He wiped the sweat from his face with his shirtsleeve.

'He reminds me of a guy I met many years ago. He died. A shame, as I'd have really liked to kill him again. Nowadays, now I'm older, I'm assailed by these memories, incredibly clear ones, of things that have happened. As if someone were inside my head, someone who had been passing the time leafing through an old photo album.'

They had been walking for hours along the dry riverbed. Monte had been summoned by a general, one of his companions from those fighting days, who had bought a huge estate near there to pass on to his daughter. He'd had a solid barrier put up around the property, cutting off the traditional grazing routes of the Mucubal shepherds. Gunshots were exchanged. A shepherd was wounded. The following night a group of young Mucubals attacked the farm, making off with a fourteen-year-old boy, the general's grandson, as well as some twenty head of cattle.

Monte took two steps towards the old man.

'May I see your wrist? Your right wrist?'

The old man was wearing a simple piece of cloth, tied at his waist, in a variety of shades of red and orange. He wore dozens of necklaces, his wrists were adorned with bright, broad copper bracelets. Monte held his arm. He was about to push up the bracelets when the blow knocked him down. The lad sitting beside the old man had leapt to his feet, throwing a violent punch at his chest. The detective fell on his back. He turned. He crawled away a few metres, coughing, trying to recover his breath, as well as his poise, while behind him a fierce argument was breaking out. Finally, he managed to get back up onto his feet. The commotion had brought people over. Young people with lustrous, rust-coloured skin were emerging from the splendour of the evening, like a miracle, gathering around the old man. They were shaking long sticks. They were rehearsing dance steps. They were leaping about. Shouting. The guide drew back, terrified:

'This is getting ugly, man. Let's get out of here!'

Back in Luanda, sat at a bar table, Monte was summarising the humiliating defeat in between gulps of beer, resorting to an image that was expressive, if inelegant:

'We were run out of there like dogs. I swallowed so much dust I've been crapping bricks ever since.'

IN WHICH A DISAPPEARANCE
IS CLEARED UP (ALMOST TWO),
OR HOW, TO QUOTE MARX:
ALL THAT IS SOLID MELTS INTO AIR

Magno Moreira Monte had woken up, on a lightless morning, feeling like a river that had lost its source. Out there, a gentle rain was dying. His wife was combing her hair, in panties and sandals, sitting on the bed.

'It's over,' said Monte. 'I can't take it any more.'

Maria Clara looked at him with a mother's calm:

'That's just as well, my love. So we can be happy now.'

That was in 2003. The new directions being taken by the party appalled him. He didn't approve of the abandoning of the old ideals, the surrender to market economics, the cosying up to capitalist powers. He quit the intelligence services and restarted his life as a private detective. Clients sought him out, on the advice of common friends, in search of information about competing firms, substantial thefts, missing persons. He received visits, too, from desperate women, looking for evidence of their husbands' betrayals, and jealous husbands, offering him considerable sums to watch their wives. Monte didn't accept these kinds of commissions, which he called, contemptuously, 'bed business'. He would recommend other colleagues.

One afternoon, the wife of a well-known businessman appeared in his office. She sat down, crossed and uncrossed her magnificent legs, like Sharon Stone in *Basic Instinct*, and shot out in a single breath:

'I want you to kill my husband.'

'What?!'

'Slowly. Very slowly.'

Monte leaned forward in his chair. He looked at her in silence for a long moment, expecting to break her. The woman didn't lower her eyes.

'I'll give you a hundred thousand dollars.'

Monte knew the businessman in question, an unscrupulous opportunist who had begun to fill his pockets back in the Marxist days, stealing, here and there, from public works.

'It's a lot of money for such a small job.'

'So you accept?'

'Why do you want to kill him?'

'I'm fed up with his betrayals. I want to see him dead. Do you accept?'

'No.'

'You don't accept?'

'No. I don't accept. I'd kill him without the slightest remorse – with a certain amount of pleasure, even, especially if it's slowly, but you haven't given me the proper motive.'

The woman left, furious. Weeks later the newspapers reported the businessman's death. He had been shot, in his car, while resisting an attempted robbery.

Monte couldn't help but smile when he heard occasional comments about the disappearance of Simon-Pierre Mulamba.

People who saw him smiling took it badly. They believed that he, an obstinate Marxist, a sceptic by nature and by training, was smiling at popular superstition. At the time, he had been annoyed at the failure of the operation. He could not bear mistakes, his own or other people's, even though the final result of the whole mix-up had pleased him. Finally, he resigned. 'That was the straw that broke the back of my infinite patience,' he explained to a friend. The war had ended. In the hotels of Luanda, businessmen from Portugal, Brazil, South Africa and Israel all rubbed shoulders, in search of quick money in a country going through a process of frantic reconstruction. From upstairs – some lavish, air-conditioned office – the order had come to silence a journalist, Daniel Benchimol, who was a specialist in disappearances. Benchimol had spent weeks questioning pilots, mechanics, businessmen, whores, travelling salesmen, opposition politicians and government ones, too, all kinds of people, about the vanishing of a Boeing 727. The plane vanished at daybreak, forty-five tons of solid metal, a wonder that nobody could explain.

'All that is solid melts into air,' muttered Monte, thinking about Marx, and thinking, like Marx, not about planes but about the capitalist system, which there in Angola, thriving like mould amid ruins, had already begun to rot everything, to corrupt everything and, thus, to bring about its own end.

Monte knew the journalist. He thought him an honest guy, even idealistic, in a field where many others chose to sell their souls to the Devil. The reports Benchimol put his name to, which were tempered by just a touch of humour, irritated and troubled the new bourgeoisie. He was descended from

Moroccan Jews who'd settled in Benguela in the middle of the nineteenth century, subsequently becoming Christianised and mulattised. His grandfather, Alberto Benchimol, a much-loved and well-respected doctor, had belonged to the 'Kuribeka', the name given to Angola's freemasons. The word comes from the Ovimbundu, and means to introduce oneself or offer oneself. The Kuribeka was established around 1860, with lodges in Benguela, Catumbela and Moçâmedes, and seems to have inspired a number of uprisings of a nationalist bent. The young man had inherited his grandfather's openness and directness, qualities Monte admired. When he received the order to silence him, the detective couldn't contain his disgust:

'This country's turned inside out. The just pay for the sinners.'

This observation, made out loud in a confident voice in front of two generals, did not go down well. One of them straightened up:

'The world has changed. The party knew how to progress along with the world, to modernise, and that's why we're still here. You ought to give some thought, comrade, to the historical process. Study a bit. How many years have you been working with us? Forever, right? I think it's too late for you to turn against us.'

The second general shrugged:

'Comrade Monte likes being provocative. He's always been like that, an agent provocateur. Just his style.'

Monte got into line. Obeying orders. Giving orders. That was all a life added up to, after all. He had the journalist watched. He discovered that every Saturday Benchimol would hire a bungalow at a small lodge in Barra do Kwanza, to meet the wife of a well-known politician. He would arrive around four. The lover would arrive an hour later, and she never stayed long. The man, though, allowed himself to linger till morning, have some breakfast, and only then would he return home.

It's routines that give the prey away.

One of Monte's best friends collected snakes and palm trees. Uli Pollak had disembarked in Luanda just a few months after Independence, on loan to the Angolan revolution from the Ministerium für Staatssicherheit. He married a woman from Benguela fifteen years his junior, with whom he had two children, and, after the collapse of the GDR, he requested and was granted Angolan citizenship. A discreet man of few words, he had earned his living producing and dealing in porcelain roses. He had built a house next to Stag Hill, with a round veranda, as vast as a plaza, almost all of it overlooking the water. It was there, as the sea swallowed up the darkness, that he received his friend, the two of them sitting outside in comfortable wicker chairs. They were drinking beer. They discussed the situation in Angola, the invasion of Iraq, the chaotic state of the city. Uli waited till the darkness had overtaken everything:

'You didn't come here to talk about the state of the traffic.'

'You're right. I need one of your snakes.'

'I knew the day would come when you'd show up to ask for something of that sort. I like my snakes. They aren't weapons.'

'I'm well aware of that. This will be the last favour I ask you. A lot of people mocked you when you decided to restart your life as a florist. It was a good decision.'

155

'You could do the same.'

'With flowers? I don't know anything about flowers.'

'Flowers. Bakeries. Nurseries. Funeral services. In this country everything is just starting up. Any business can work out.'

'Business?' Monte laughed. An embittered laugh. 'I have no talent for multiplying money. I can ruin the very best businesses. I'll never be more than just about able to scrape by, I've already resigned myself to that. So, anyway, give me the snake, and forget the whole thing.'

The following night, one of his men, a solid guy from Malange, armour-plated, whom they called Kissonde, made his way over to the lodge where Daniel Benchimol stayed. It was after midnight. It was raining lightly. Kissonde knocked on the door to bungalow number six. A tall, handsome mulatto man opened it. He was in a nice-looking pair of silk pyjamas, in a metallic blue with white stripes. The agent pointed a pistol at him, while at the same time bringing his left index finger to his lips in an expressive gesture:

'*Sssshhhhh*. Not one word. I don't want you to get hurt.' He pushed the mulatto inside and made him sit on the bed. Then, never diverting the threat of the pistol, he drew a bottle of pills from his jacket pocket.

'You're going to swallow two. Lie down and you'll sleep like a baby. Tomorrow you'll wake up perfectly happy, just a little bit poorer.'

According to the plan, Daniel Benchimol would swallow the pills, and then, after just a few minutes, he would fall asleep. Kissonde was then to put on a pair of thick leather gloves, take from his rucksack a coral snake, which had come from old Uli, grip it by the head and bring it over to bite the journalist. He would then depart nice and quietly, without anyone seeing him, leaving the snake in the bedroom. The following morning a cleaning woman would come upon the dead body, the snake, the bottle of pills, and sound the alarm. A lot of shouting, a lot of weeping. Fine speeches at the funeral. A perfect crime.

Unfortunately, the mulatto refused to stick to the script. Rather than swallowing the pills and falling asleep, he let out a swear word in French, threw the bottle onto the floor, and was about to get up when Kissonde struck him violently, knocking him down. The man was sprawled across the bed, passed out, with split lips, bleeding heavily. Kissonde proceeded with his plan. He forced the pills down his throat, put on the gloves, opened the rucksack, took hold of the snake by the head and made it bite the mulatto's neck. It was then that another unexpected occurrence took place. The snake clasped itself furiously onto the agent's nose. Kissonde grabbed hold of it, pulled at it, but the animal didn't let go. Finally he managed to yank it off. He threw it onto the floor, stamping on it several times. He sat down on the bed, trembling, took his cell phone out of the rucksack and called Monte:

'Boss, we've got a situation.'

Monte, who was waiting for him in the car at the entrance to the lodge, raced over to bungalow number six. The door was closed. He knocked lightly. Nobody came to open it. He knocked harder. The door opened and he was met by the sight of – dishevelled, in underpants, radiating health – Daniel Benchimol.

'Sorry, are you alright?'

The journalist rubbed his eyes, startled:

'Shouldn't I be?'

Monte made up a hasty excuse, another guest had heard a cry, maybe nightbirds going after their prey, a cat in heat, rogue nightmares, excused himself again, wished the astonished journalist a quiet remainder of his night and moved away. He called up Kissonde:

'Where the hell have you got to?'

He heard a moan. A voice crumbling:

'I'm dying, boss. Come quick.'

Monte had a brainwave. He ran over to bungalow number nine. He found that the metal number had indeed come loose at the top, and had swung down to form a number six. The door was just pushed to. He went in. Kissonde was sitting facing the door, his face swollen, nose even more swollen, eyelids drooping:

'I'm dying, boss,' he said, slowly holding up his hands in a gesture of helplessness. 'The snake bit me.'

Behind him, Monte saw another guy, bleeding from his mouth.

'Fuck, Kissonde! What about that guy? Who's he?'

He went straight over to a jacket hanging on the back of a chair, beside the desk. He rifled through the pockets. He found a wallet and a passport.

'French! Holy shit, Kissonde, you've killed a Frenchman!'

He fetched the jeep. He sat Kissonde at shotgun. He was about to drag out the inanimate body of Simon-Pierre when he was surprised by one of the lodge's guards.

'Well now!' sighed Monte. A bit of good luck amid the bad. The man had worked with him in the hard years. The guard stood to attention:

'Commander!'

He helped Monte put Simon-Pierre on the back seat of the jeep. He brought clean sheets. They made the bed. They cleaned the room. They put the snake (what was left of it) into Kissonde's rucksack. When Monte was just about to leave, after handing the guard a hundred dollars to make it easier for him to forget the whole episode, he spotted the felt hat the Frenchman had worn as he wandered around Luanda.

'I'm taking the hat. I'll take some clothes, too. Nobody goes missing in their pyjamas.'

He dropped Kissonde at the military hospital. He drove an hour to a piece of land he had bought years earlier, having intended to build there, far from the noise of Luanda, a wooden house, painted blue, where he and his wife would face their old age. He parked the jeep beside an enormous baobab. It was a lovely night, lit by a copper moon, round and tight as the skin of a drum. He took a shovel from the trunk and opened a grave in the soft earth, wet from the rain. An old Chico Buarque song came to his mind: '*This grave where you lie | measured out by hand | is the smallest expense you ever claimed from the land | the grave is a good size | not too deep a foundation | it's the part that falls to you of this whole plantation.*' He leaned up against the baobab, humming: '*The grave is very large | for your corpse off its bier | but you'll be a bigger man | than you ever were here.*'

In the penultimate year of high school, in the city of Huambo, he had joined an amateur theatre group that had staged *The*

Death and Life of Severino, a play with words by João Cabral de Melo Neto and music by Chico Buarque. The experience changed how he looked at the world. He understood, as he played the part of a poor peasant from the Brazilian north-east, the contradictions and injustices of the colonial system. In April 1974 he was in Lisbon, studying law, when the streets were filled with red carnations. He bought a ticket and returned to Luanda to start a revolution. So many years had gone by, and there he was, humming 'The Labourer's Funeral' while he buried, in an unmarked grave, a writer who hadn't had luck on his side.

He re-entered Luanda at four in the morning. He was thinking about what he might do next, how to justify the disappearance of the Frenchman, when, just as he was passing the Quinaxixe market, inspiration struck. He parked the car, and got out. He took the dead man's hat and made his way round to the back of a building, next door to a nightclub, the Quizás, Quizás, where Simon-Pierre had been that night. He put the hat down on the damp ground. There was a kid asleep next to a dumpster. He woke him with a thump:

'Did you see that?!'

The boy leapt up, confused.

'See what, old man?'

'There, where that hat is! There was a tall mulatto, taking a leak, and then all of a sudden the earth swallowed him up. It only left the hat.'

The boy turned his big spotty face to him. He opened his eyes wide:

'Whoa, man! Did you really see it?'

'I did, clear as day. Earth swallowed him up. First there was a glow of light, then nothing. Just the hat.'

They stood there, the two of them, stunned, contemplating the hat. Their amazement caught the attention of three other kids, who approached, looking both fearful and defiant:

'What's happened, Baiacu?'

Baiacu turned to face them, triumphant. In the days that followed, people would listen to him. People would crowd around him to hear what he had to say. A man with a good story is practically a king.

SABALU AND HIS DEAD

On the day Sabalu broke through the wall, Ludo confessed her greatest nightmare to him: she had killed a man and buried him on the terrace. The boy listened to her without surprise.

'That was a long time ago, grandma. Even he doesn't remember that now.'

'He who?'

'Your dead man, that Trinitá. My mum used to say that the dead suffer from amnesia. They suffer even more because of the poor memories of the living. You remember him every day, and that's good. You should laugh as you remember him, you should dance. You need to talk to Trinitá the way you talk to Phantom. Talking calms the dead.'

'Did you learn that from your mother, too?'

'Yes. My mother died on me when I was a child. I was left abandoned. I talk to her, but I haven't got those hands protecting me now.'

'You're still a child.'

'I can't do it, grandma. How can I be a child if I'm far from my mother's arms?'

'I'll give you mine.'

Ludo hadn't hugged anyone in a long time. She was a bit out of practice, and Sabalu had to lift her arms up. It was really him making a nest for himself on the old lady's lap. Only later did he talk about his mother, a nurse, killed for fighting against the trade in human corpses. In the hospital where she worked, in a city in the north, corpses would sometimes disappear. Some of the employees used to sell the organs to the witch doctors, thereby increasing their meagre salaries fivefold. Filomena, Sabalu's mother, had begun by rebelling against the corrupt employees, later moving on to fight the witch doctors, too. She started having problems. A car burst out at her as she was leaving work, almost running her over. Her house was burgled five times. They left charms nailed to her door, notes with insults and threats. None of this deterred her. One October morning, in the market, a man approached her and stabbed her in the stomach. Sabalu saw his mother drop to the ground. He heard her voice, in a hiss:

'Just run for it, son!'

Filomena had arrived pregnant from São Tomé, attracted by the bright eyes, the broad shoulders, the easy laugh and the warm voice of a young officer in the Angolan Armed Forces. The officer had taken her from Luanda to that city in the north, he had lived with her for eight months, been there for Sabalu's birth, then gone off on a mission to the south, which was supposed to last just a few days, but he'd never come back.

The boy ran across the market, knocking over baskets of fruit, crates of beer, chirping wicker cages. A violent commotion of protest was erupting behind him. Sabalu didn't stop till he had arrived home. He stood there, at a loss, not knowing what to do. Then the door opened and a crooked man, dressed in black, pounced on him like a bird of prey. The boy dodged him, rolled over on the tarmac, got up, and without looking back, broke into a run again.

A truck driver agreed to take him to Luanda. Sabalu told him the truth: his mother had died, and his father had disappeared. He hoped that once in the capital he'd be able to track down someone from his family. He knew his father's name was Marciano Barroso, that he was, or had been, a captain in the Armed Forces, and that he'd disappeared on a mission somewhere in the south. He knew, too, that his father was a native of Luanda. His paternal grandparents lived on the big Quinaxixe plaza. He remembered hearing his mother mention the name. She'd told him that there, on that big plaza, a lagoon had grown, with dark waters, where a mermaid lived.

The truck driver dropped him at Quinaxixe. He put a wad of banknotes in Sabalu's pocket:

'This money should be enough for you to rent a room for a week, and to eat and drink. I hope you find your father in the meantime.'

The boy roamed around, distressed, for hours and hours. He first approached an obese policeman positioned outside the door to a bank:

'Please, sir, do you know Captain Barroso?'

The policeman fired a gaze at him, eyes sparkling with rage:

'Move on, layabout, move on!'

A woman selling vegetables took pity on the boy. She stopped a moment to hear him out. She called over some others.

One of them remembered an old man, one Adão Barroso, who had lived in the Cuca building. He'd died years ago.

It was already getting late when hunger drove Sabalu into a small bar. He sat down, fearful. He ordered a soup and a Coke. When he left, a lad with a swollen face, his skin in very poor shape, shoved him against the wall:

'My name's Baiacu, kid. I'm the King of Quinaxixe.' He pointed at the statue of a woman in the middle of the park. 'She's my queen. Her, Queen Ginga. Me, King Gingão. You got any cash?'

Sabalu shrunk back, crying. Two other boys emerged from the shadows, flanking Baiacu, preventing his flight. They were identical, short and solid, like pit bulls, dull eyes and the same engrossed smile on well-drawn lips. Sabalu put his hand in his pocket and showed him the money. Baiacu snatched the notes:

'Ace, pal. Tonight you can crib with us, over there, where the boxes are. We'll look out for you. Tomorrow you start work. What's your name?'

'Sabalu.'

'A pleasure, Sabalu. This is Diogo!'

'Which one?'

'Both. Diogo is both of them.'

It took Sabalu some time to understand that the two bodies constituted a single person. They moved about in unison, or rather, vibrated in harmony, like synchronised swimmers. They spoke, simultaneously, the same few words. They laughed common laughs. They wept identical tears. Pregnant women fainted when they saw Diogo. Children ran from him. Diogo himself, however, seemed not to have the least vocation for malice. He had the goodness of a Surinam cherry tree, which bears fruit in the sun, albeit discreet and infrequent, more out of negligence than any clear determination of the spirit. Baiacu had earned himself some money by making Diogo sing and dance *kuduru* outside the big hotels. The foreigners were fascinated. They would leave generous tips. One Portuguese journalist wrote a small article about the *kudurista*, which included a photograph of Diogo, his arms around Baiacu. Baiacu always carried a cutting of the article in his trouser pocket. He'd look proud:

'I'm a street-businessman.'

Sabalu started out by washing cars. He would hand the money over to Baiacu. The street-businessman bought food for everyone. For himself he also bought cigarettes and beer. Sometimes he'd drink too much. He'd become a talker. He would philosophise:

'The truth is the sole-less shoe of a man who doesn't know how to lie.'

He became easily irritated. On one occasion, Diogo allowed some other boys to steal a small battery-powered radio that Baiacu had managed to extract from the back seat of a jeep that was stuck in traffic. That night Baiacu lit a fire by the side of the lagoon. He heated up a sheet of iron till it was red-hot. He called Diogo over, grabbed one of his hands and held it to the metal plate. Both Diogo's bodies twisted desperately. Both his mouths gave a high-pitched howl. Sabalu threw up, tortured by the smell of burned flesh and Diogo's desperation.

'You're weak,' spat Baiacu. 'You'll never be king.'

From that day on, to make Sabalu a man – just a man since

he'd never be able to transform him into a king – he started taking him along on short pilfering expeditions. These would happen in the late afternoons, when the bourgeois were heading home in their cars, languishing in traffic jams for hours on end. There was always some poor soul who'd roll down a window, either to let in some air because the air conditioning wasn't working, or to ask someone a question. Then Baiacu would spring out of the shadows, his face spiked with pimples, his wide eyes aflame, and hold a shard of glass to their neck. Sabalu would stick his hands through the window and take a wallet, a watch, any object of value within his reach. Then the two of them would race away into the confusion of cars and people shouting threats, and the fury of car horns, occasionally gunshots.

It had been Baiacu's idea to climb the scaffolding. He instructed Sabalu:

'You climb up, see if there's a window open anywhere and get in without making noise. I can't do it. Heights make me really sick. Also, the higher I go, the shorter I feel.'

Sabalu climbed up onto the terrace. He saw the dead chickens. He walked down the stairs and discovered an apartment that was stripped to the bone, without furniture, without doors or flooring. The walls, which were covered in inscriptions and strange drawings, scared him. He backed slowly towards the staircase. He told Baiacu there was nothing there. The next night, however, he climbed the scaffolding again. This time he ventured across the few remaining floor tiles. In the bedroom he found the old woman sleeping on a mattress, clothes in one corner. The kitchen was the only place in the house that looked normal, apart from the walls that had been blackened by smoke. There was a heavy-looking table, marble-topped, an oven and fridge. The boy took out a bread roll that he'd brought from his pocket – he always had a bread roll in his pocket – and put it on the table. In a drawer he found a set of silver cutlery. He put it in his rucksack and left. He handed the cutlery over to Baiacu. The boy was impressed, and whistled:

'Good work, kid. You didn't find any dough, any jewels?'

Sabalu said no. There was more poverty up there than down here on the streets of Luanda. Baiacu didn't agree:

'You're going back tomorrow.'

Sabalu just nodded. He asked for money to buy some bread. He put the bread, a stick of butter and a bottle of Coke into his rucksack and scaled the building. When Baiacu saw him coming back empty-handed, he exploded. He threw himself on Sabalu, punching and kicking. He knocked him down. He went on kicking his head, his neck, till Diogo held his arms and pulled him off. The following night, Sabalu climbed up to the terrace again. This time he found Ludo sprawled on the floor. He came back down, very alarmed. He asked Baiacu to let him buy medicine. The old woman had fallen over. She looked really bad. But the other boy didn't even listen:

'I don't see wings on your back, Sabalu. If you haven't got wings, you're not an angel. Let the old woman die.'

Sabalu fell silent. He accompanied Baiacu and Diogo to Roque Santeiro. They sold the cutlery. They had lunch around there, in a bar that rose up, perched on stilts, over the Babel-like confusion of the market. Sabalu let Baiacu finish his beer. Then he dared to ask whether he might have some of the money for himself. After all, he'd been the one who'd brought the cutlery. The other boy was enraged:

'What do you want the dough for? Anything you need I give you. I'm like a father to you.'

'Let me just see the money. I've never seen so much all together.'

Baiacu handed him the thick wad of banknotes. Sabalu grabbed hold of them. He jumped down from the terrace onto the sand. When he got back to his feet, his knees were bleeding. He ran, slipping through the crowds, while Baiacu, leaning over the ledge, yelled insults and threats:

'Thief! Son of a bitch! I'm going to kill you.'

Sabalu bought medicine and food. It was getting late when he returned to Quinaxixe. He saw Baiacu sitting with Diogo beside the scaffolding. He approached another kid and handed him five banknotes:

'Tell Baiacu I'm waiting for him at the Verde Bar.'

The boy ran off. He passed on the message. Baiacu leapt to his feet and went, followed by Diogo, in the opposite direction. Sabalu climbed the scaffolding. He didn't breathe easy till he had reached the terrace.

DANIEL BENCHIMOL INVESTIGATES
LUDO'S DISAPPEARANCE

Daniel Benchimol read through the letter from Maria da Piedade Lourenço twice. He phoned a friend of his father's, a geologist, who had devoted his entire life to diamond prospecting. Old Vitalino remembered Orlando very well:

'A good fellow, very ugly. Really stiff and skinny, always standing very tense, as though he were wearing a shirt with studs in it. They called him Spike. Nobody wanted to have a coffee with him. He didn't make friends. He disappeared not long before Independence. He took advantage of the chaos, stuck a few stones in his pocket, and ran off to Brazil.'

Daniel did some research online. He found hundreds of people called Orlando Pereira dos Santos. He wasted hours following every clue, any mention, that might take him from the name to the man he was after. No luck. He found it strange. A man like Orlando, living for twenty-something years in Brazil, or in any country that wasn't Afghanistan, or Sudan, or Bhutan, would have to leave some trace on the great virtual web. He called up Vitalino again:

'Did this Orlando guy have any family in Angola?'

'Probably. He was from Catete.'

'Catete? I thought he was Portuguese!'

'No, no! Catete, hundred per cent. Real light skin. After the twenty-fifth of April he insisted on reminding us of his origins. He boasted of having lived with Agostinho Neto himself. Would you believe it? A guy who all those years had never once raised his voice against colonialism. I should add, for the sake of the whole truth, that he didn't do deals with racists, he never did that. He always acted like a decent kind of guy. He acted with just the same arrogance towards both whites and blacks.'

'And his family?'

'Well then, his family. I think he was a cousin of Vitorino Gavião.'

'The poet?'

'A tramp. Call him what you like.'

Benchimol knew where to find Vitorino Gavião. He crossed the street and went into Biker. The historic beer hall was almost empty at this time of day. Sitting at one table, towards the back, four men were playing cards. They were arguing loudly. They fell silent when they saw him approach.

'Careful!' said one of them sharply, in a pretend whisper but wanting the journalist to hear him. 'The establishment press has arrived. The owner's voice. The owner's ears.'

Benchimol was annoyed:

'If I'm the voice of the regime, you're the excrement.'

The one who had whispered straightened up:

'Don't get annoyed, comrade. Have a beer.'

Vitorino Gavião let out a bitter laugh:

'We're the Greek chorus. The voice of the nation's conscience. That's what we are. Here we sit, in the gloom, passing comment on the progress of the tragedy. Giving warnings to which nobody pays heed.'

A runaway baldness had robbed him of the thick head of hair, Jimi Hendrix-style, with which in 1960s Paris he had proclaimed his *négritude*. The way he was now, his skull smooth and shining, he could pass for a white man even in Sweden. Well, perhaps not in Sweden. He raised his voice, curious:

'What's the news?'

The journalist pulled up a chair. He sat down.

'Did you know a guy called Orlando Pereira dos Santos, a mining engineer?'

Gavião hesitated, very pale:

'My cousin. First cousin. Did he die?'

'I don't know. Would you stand to gain anything from his death?'

'The guy disappeared around Independence. They say he took a package of diamonds with him.'

'You think he'd still remember you?'

'We were friends. Spike's silence in the early years didn't surprise me. If I'd stolen a package of diamonds I'd want to be forgotten, too. He was forgotten. Everybody forgot him a long time ago. Why are you asking me these questions?'

The journalist showed him the letter from Maria da Piedade Lourenço. Gavião remembered Ludo. He'd always found her a bit distracted. Now he understood why. He remembered his visits to his cousin's apartment, in the Prédio dos Invejados. The euphoria of those days before Independence.

'If I'd known how it was going to end up, I'd have stayed in Paris.'

'And what were you doing – there, in Paris?'

'Nothing,' sighed Gavião. 'Nothing, like here. But at least I was doing it elegantly. I could be a *flâneur.*'

That same afternoon, after leaving the newspaper offices, Daniel walked up to Quinaxixe. The Prédio dos Invejados still looked pretty dilapidated. Nevertheless, the entrance hall was freshly painted, and the air was clean and cheerful. A security guard was posted at the elevator.

'Does it work?' asked the journalist.

The man smiled, proudly.

'Almost always, boss, almost always!'

He asked Daniel for some identification and only then did he call the lift. The journalist got in. He went up to the eleventh floor. He got out. He paused a moment, struck by the cleanness of the walls and the shine on the floor tiles. There was only one door that jarred with the others, the door to apartment D. It was scratched and revealed a small hole, halfway up, that looked like a bullet wound. The journalist pressed the doorbell. He didn't hear a sound. Then he knocked three times, hard. A boy came to the door. Big eyes, a mature expression surprising in someone so young.

'Hello,' the journalist greeted him. 'Do you live here?'

'Yes, sir, I do. Me and my grandma.'

'Can I talk to your grandma?'

'No.'

'Let be, son, I'll talk to him.'

Daniel heard the voice, fragile, cracked, and only then saw

the very pale woman appear, dragging one leg, her grey hair parted into two thick braids.

'I am Ludovica Fernandes, my good man. What do you want?'

MUTIATI BLUES (2)

The old man watched as January rose up and closed in around the Kuvale people like a trap. First the drought. A lot of oxen died. The further east they travelled, climbing the range of hills, the sweeter the air became, the ground getting cooler and softer. They found some pasture, muddy watering holes, and they walked on, struggling to decipher the faint hints of green. The fence just popped up by surprise, like an insult, offending the luminous hip of the morning. The herd came to a stop. The young men gathered in nervous groups, calling out sharply in surprise and indignation. António, the son, came over. He was sweating. His handsome face, with its straight nose, its prominent chin, was flushed through effort and rage:

'What do we do now?'

The old man sat down. The fence ran for hundreds of metres. To the right it emerged from a harsh tangle of bramble bushes, which the locals called cat's claws, and to the left it plunged into an even thicker, more sharply pointed nightmare of wild bushes, of long cacti in the shape of candelabra, and of mutiati trees. Beyond the barrier was a soft path of white pebbles, along which, at that time of year, a small brook was meant to be flowing.

Jeremias Carrasco selected a twig, smoothed out the sand, and began to write. António crouched beside him.

That afternoon they knocked down the fence and crossed to the other side. They found a bit of water. Good pastures. The wind began to blow. It carried heavy shadows along with it, as though it were carrying the night, in shreds, yanked away from some other, even more distant desert. They heard the sound of an engine and saw, appearing through the gloom and the dust, a jeep carrying six armed men. One of them, a skinny mulatto with the destitute look of a wet cat, leapt from the car and came towards them waving an AK-47 in his right hand.

He was shouting in Portuguese and Nkumbi. A few phrases, torn to pieces by the wind, reached Jeremias's ears:

'This is private land! Get out! Get out now!'

The old man raised his right hand, trying to hold back the momentum of the young men. Too late. A lanky young lad, who had only just taken a wife, and whom they called Zebra, threw a small assegai. The spear traced an elegant arc in the panicky sky and planted itself, with a dry crunch, just centimetres from the mulatto's boots.

There was the briefest moment of silence. The very wind seemed to abate. Then the guard raised his gun and fired.

In the harsh light of midday it would have been a bloodbath. The six men were armed. Some of the shepherds had been in the military, and they too were carrying firearms. At that time, however, with the wind whipping through the darkness, only two bullets found their way into flesh. Zebra was lightly wounded in one arm. The mulatto in a leg. Both parties drew back, but in the confusion a lot of cows were left behind.

The following night, a group of young shepherds, led by Zebra, went back to the estate. They returned with some of the missing cattle, half a dozen cows that didn't belong to them, and a fourteen-year-old boy, who, according to Zebra, had chased after them on horseback, shouting like a man possessed.

Jeremias was alarmed. Stealing cattle is tradition. It happens all the time. In this case, it was a kind of exchange. The kidnapping of the boy, though, that really could cause them some problems. The old man sent for him. He was an adolescent with very green eyes, untamed hair tied into a ponytail. One of those characters who in Angola are often called 'lost frontiers', because by daylight they look white, and at twilight they are discovered in fact to be part mulatto – from which it might be concluded that sometimes you can understand people better further away from the light. The boy looked at the old man with contempt:

'My granddad is going to kill you!'

Jeremias laughed. He wrote in the sand:

I've died once before. Second time won't be so bad.

The boy stammered something, surprised. He started to cry.

'I'm André Ruço, *senhor*. I'm General Ruço's grandson. Tell them not to hurt me. Let me go. Keep the cows but let me go.'

The old man made an effort to persuade the young ones to release André. They demanded their cows back and a guarantee that they could cross the estate in search of better pastures. They'd been at this for three days when Jeremias saw the past crouching down before him. It had aged, which doesn't always

185

happen – sometimes the past travels centuries without time corrupting it at all. Not this time: this man had withered even more, he had more wrinkles, and what hair he had left was practically colourless. His voice, though, remained solid and firm. At that moment, when Jeremias found himself faced with Monte, seeing him stand up and get pushed backwards, seeing him run off, chased by the young shepherds, he was reminded of Orlando Pereira dos Santos and his diamonds.

THE STRANGE DESTINY OF
THE KUBANGO RIVER

Nasser Evangelista was pleased with his new job. He wore a blue uniform, very clean, and spent most of his time sitting at a desk, reading, while he watched the door out the corner of his eye. He had developed his taste for reading during the years he'd spent locked up in the São Paulo prison in Luanda. After his release, he'd worked as a craftsman, carving masks in the Mile-Eleven Market. One afternoon he met Little Chief, with whom he'd shared a cell, who invited him to work as a doorman at the Prédio dos Invejados at Quinaxixe, where the businessman had just moved in.

'It's a quiet job,' he assured him. 'You'll be able to read.'

With this, he persuaded him. That morning, Nasser Evangelista was rereading, for the seventh time, the adventures of Robinson Crusoe when he noticed a very ugly boy, his face pitted with acne, lurking around the entrance to the building. Nasser marked his page and put the book away in a drawer. He got up, and walked over to the door:

'Hey, you! Spotty kid! What do you want with my building?'

The lad approached, intimidated:

'Do you know if there's a boy living here?'

'Several, kid. This building's a whole city.'

'A seven-year-old boy, name's Sabalu.'

'Ah, yes! Sabalu, I know the one. Eleven-E. Very nice kid. Lives with his grandmother, but I've never seen her. She doesn't leave the house.'

At that moment, two other characters appeared. Nasser was startled to see them walking up the road, both dressed in black, as though they had stepped straight out of an adventure from *Corto Maltese*. The older of the two wore a Mucubal hat, with red and yellow stripes, necklaces around his neck and big bracelets on his wrists. He was wearing old leather sandals, which revealed huge feet that were cracked and covered in dust. Next to the old man, moving with the elegance of someone showing himself on a catwalk, was a young man, very tall and thin. He, too, had bracelets and necklaces, but on him such accessories seemed as natural as the bowler hat that covered his head. The two men were walking decisively towards Nasser. 'We're going up,' the young man informed him, while with a gesture of annoyance he pushed the doorman aside. Nasser had received very firm instructions that he was not to allow anyone in without first taking a note of the number on their ID card or driver's licence. He was about to block their way when Baiacu, dodging around him, dashed off up the stairs. The doorman followed him. Jeremias and his son called the elevator, got in, and rode it up. When they got out on the eleventh floor, the old man had a dizzy spell. He couldn't catch his breath. He leaned against the wall for a moment. He saw Daniel Benchimol, who was greeting

Ludo, and he recognised her, even though he had never met her before.

'I have a letter for you,' Daniel was saying. 'Perhaps it would be better if we went inside, so you can sit down and we might talk.'

While this was happening, Magno Moreira Monte was coming into the building. He didn't find the doorman, so he called the elevator and went up. He heard Nasser's shouts as he chased Baiacu:

'Come back. You can't go up there!'

Little Chief, who was at home shaving, was also alarmed at the doorman's shouts. He washed his face, put on some trousers, and went to the door to look into the hallway and see what the commotion was about. Baiacu ran past him, pushed the shepherds aside and stopped just a few metres away from Daniel Benchimol. Then at once the elevator door opened and the ex-prisoner was surprised to find himself face to face with the man who, twenty-five years back, had questioned and tortured him.

Baiacu took a switchblade from his trouser pocket, flicked it open and showed it to Sabalu:

'Thief! I'm going to cut your ears off!'

The boy faced up to him:

'Come on, then. I'm not scared of you any more!'

Ludo pushed him into the apartment:

'Go in, child. We were wrong to open the door.'

Nasser Evangelista fell onto Baiacu and disarmed him:

'Easy, kid, drop that now. We're going to have a talk.'

Monte was pleased to see Little Chief's astonishment:

'Ah, comrade Arnaldo Cruz! Whenever I hear anyone speaking ill of Angola, I always use you as an example. A country in which even the madmen get rich, even the enemies of the regime, does necessarily have to be a pretty generous one!'

António, stunned at the collection of events, whispered into the old man's ear, in the twisting language of the Kuvale:

'These people don't have oxen, father. They know nothing about oxen.'

Daniel Benchimol held Ludo's arm:

'Wait a moment, ma'am. Read the letter.'

Little Chief stuck an index finger into Monte's chest:

'What are you laughing at, you hyena? The hyenas' days are over now.'

Ludo handed back the envelope:

'My eyes are no longer any use for reading.'

Monte pushed Little Chief's arm away, and as he turned his body he noticed Jeremias. This coincidence seemed to please him even more:

'Well, now, another familiar face. That meeting of ours out in Namibe didn't go too well. Not for me, at least. But this time, you people are on my turf.'

Daniel Benchimol shuddered when he heard Monte's voice. He turned to the detective:

'I'm just starting to remember you myself, sir. You woke me on the night Simon-Pierre disappeared. The idea was to make me disappear, not him – right?'

At this point, all eyes were on the old agent. Nasser Evangelista let go of Baiacu and advanced on Monte, enraged, the knife in the air:

'I remember you, too, sir, and they are not happy memories.'

Finding himself surrounded by Jeremias, António, Little Chief, Daniel Benchimol and Nasser Evangelista, Monte began to back towards the staircase:

'Take it easy, take it easy – what happened, happened. We're all of us Angolans.'

Nasser Evangelista didn't hear him. He heard only his own cries, a quarter of a century earlier, in a narrow cell that stank of shit and piss. He heard the cries of a woman he never saw, coming from some other identical darkness. Shouts, and the barking of dogs. Behind him everything was shouting. Everything was barking. He took two steps forward and pressed the blade to Monte's chest. He was surprised to meet no resistance. He repeated the gesture again and again. The detective staggered, very pale, and brought his hands up to his shirt. He saw no blood. His clothes were intact. Jeremias took Nasser by the shoulders and pulled him towards him. Daniel grabbed the knife from his hand.

'It's fake, thank God. It's a circus knife.'

So it was. The knife had a hollow handle, with a spring, into which the blade slid, disappearing when something pushed against it.

Daniel stabbed himself in the chest and the neck to demonstrate to the others the fakeness of the weapon. Then he leaped onto Jeremias. He stabbed Nasser. He laughed loud, big, hysterical laughter, and the others joined in. Ludo laughed too, holding on to Sabalu, tears running from her eyes.

Only Monte remained serious. He smoothed out his shirt, straightened his back, walked down the stairs. Outside, the air burned. A dry wind shook the trees. The detective struggled to breathe. His chest hurt, not where Nasser had struck those fictional knife-blows, but inside, in some secret place, somewhere he couldn't name. He wiped his eyes. He took the dark glasses from his trouser pocket and put them on. He recalled, for no apparent reason, the image of a canoe floating in the Okavango Delta.

The Kubango starts being called the Okavango when it crosses the Namibian border. Though it is a large river, it doesn't fulfill the same destiny as its peers: it doesn't empty into the sea. It opens its broad arms and dies in the middle of the desert. It is a sublime death, a generous one, which fills the sands of the Kalahari with green and with life. Monte had spent his thirtieth wedding anniversary on the Okavango Delta, in an eco-lodge – a gift from his children. Those had been blessed days, he and Maria Clara catching beetles and butterflies, reading, going on canoe trips.

There are some people who experience a fear of being forgotten. It's a pathology called athazagoraphobia. The opposite happened to him, he lived in terror that he would never be forgotten. There, on the Okavango Delta, he had felt forgotten. He had been happy.

IN WHICH IT IS REVEALED
HOW NASSER EVANGELISTA
HELPED LITTLE CHIEF TO
ESCAPE FROM PRISON

We always die of dejection. That is, when our souls fail us, then we die. That was Little Chief's theory. In support of this, the businessman described what had happened to him the second time he was arrested. He'd faced the terrible prison conditions, the ill treatment, the torture, with a courage that surprised not only his companions in misfortune but also the prison guards and the agents of the political police.

It wasn't courage, he admitted:

'I was experiencing serious rebelliousness. My soul was rebelling against the injustices. Fear, yes, the fear came to hurt me more than the blows, but the rebellion was outgrowing the fear, and that was when I confronted the police. I was never quiet. When they shouted at me, I shouted louder. At a certain point, I realised those guys were more scared of me than I was of them.'

One time when they were punishing him, and they put him in a tiny cell, which they called Kifangondo after the site of the great battle, Little Chief found a rat and adopted it. He called it Splendour, a name that was perhaps a little optimistic for a common rat, brown and shifty, with a gnawed-on ear and fur in pretty poor shape. When Little Chief reappeared in the regular cell, with Splendour nestled on his right shoulder, some of his companions teased him. Most ignored him. At that time, at the end of the seventies, the São Paulo prison brought together an extraordinary collection of personalities. American and English mercenaries, taken in combat, lived alongside dissident exiles from the ANC who had fallen into misfortune. Young intellectuals from the far left exchanged ideas with old Portuguese Salazarists. There were guys locked up for diamond trafficking, and others for not having stood to attention during the raising of the flag. Some of the prisoners had been important leaders in the party. They took pride in their friendship with the president.

'Only yesterday, the old man and I went fishing together,' one of them boasted to Little Chief. 'When he finds out what's happened he'll get me out of here and have the morons who did this to me arrested.'

He was shot the following week.

Many didn't even know what they'd been accused of. Some went crazy. The interrogations often seemed erratic, preposterous, as though the aim were not to extract information from the detainees, but merely to torture and confuse them.

In this context, a man with a trained rat wasn't enough to surprise anyone. Little Chief took care of Splendour. He taught him tricks. He'd say 'Sit!', and the animal sat. 'Around!', he'd order, and the rat started walking in circles. Monte heard about this and went to the cell to visit the prisoner.

'They tell me you've made a new friend.'

Little Chief didn't answer. He'd created a rule for himself never to reply to an agent from the political police, unless the agent was shouting. In such cases he would scream an attack at him in return, accusing him of being in the service of the socio-fascist dictatorship, etc. Monte found the prisoner's behaviour exasperating:

'I'm talking to you, for fuck's sake! Don't act like I'm invisible.'

Little Chief turned his back on him. Monte lost it, and tugged on his shirt. That was the moment he saw Splendour. He grabbed hold of the animal, threw it onto the floor and stamped on it. In the midst of all those crimes, the vast crimes that were being committed in those days, right there, within the prison walls, the tiny death of Splendour affected nobody, apart from Little Chief. The young man fell into deep dejection. He spent his days lying on a mat, unspeaking, unmoving, indifferent to his cellmates. He became so thin that his ribs stuck out beneath his skin like the keys of a *kisanji*. Finally, they took him to the infirmary.

When he was arrested, Nasser Evangelista had been working at the Maria Pia hospital as an orderly. He took no interest in politics. All his attention was trained on a young nurse called Sueli Mirela, well known for the length of her legs, which she displayed generously in daring miniskirts, and for her round hairdo in the style of Angela Davis. The girl, who was going out with a state security agent, allowed herself to be seduced by the orderly's sweet words. Her boyfriend, in a rage, accused his rival of being linked to the fractionists. When he was locked up, Nasser started to work in the prison infirmary. He was moved when he saw Little Chief's condition. He conceived and organised the plan himself, a plan that was brave and yet happy, which made it possible to return the frail young man to freedom. Well, to relative freedom since, as Little Chief himself liked to repeat, no man is free as long as one other man is in prison.

Nasser Evangelista registered the death of Little Chief, alias Arnaldo Cruz, aged nineteen, student of law, and he himself put the body in the coffin. A distant cousin, who was in reality a comrade from the same small party in which he was himself an activist, received the casket. He buried it, in a discreet ceremony at the Alto das Cruzes cemetery. He did this after removing the passenger in question. Little Chief got into the habit of visiting the grave on the anniversary of his supposed death, taking flowers to himself. 'To me, it's a reflection on the fragility of life and a small exercise in otherness,' he explained to his friends. 'I go out there, and I try and think of myself as a close relative. I am, really, my own closest relative. I think about his defects, about his qualities, and whether or not he deserves my tears. I almost always cry a little.'

It was months before the police discovered the fraud. Then they arrested him again.

MYSTERIES OF LUANDA

Little Chief enjoyed talking to the handicraft sellers. He would get lost down the dusty alleyways amid the wooden stalls, studying the Congolese fabrics, the thousand and one cloths showing sunsets and drums, the Chokwe masks the crafts-men used to bury, during the rainy months, to make them look old. Sometimes he'd buy some object or other he didn't even like, just to prolong the conversation. Moved more by a spirit of solidarity than any thought of financial gain, he set up a company to produce and trade in handicrafts. He would imagine and design pieces in dark wood, which the craftsmen then undertook to replicate. He sold the objects at Luanda airport and in small shops dedicated to so-called 'fair trade', in Paris, London and New York. He employed more than twenty craftsmen. One of the most successful pieces was the figure of a Thinker, a popular figure of traditional Angolan statuary, with a gag over his mouth. The people named it *Don't Think*.

One afternoon, Little Chief walked across the market without paying much attention to the sellers. He just smiled, nodding at anyone who greeted him. Papy Bolingô was beginning his show. Fofo was singing an old number by Orchestra Baobab. The bar was full. Seeing him arrive, one of the staff came over to him carrying a folding chair. He opened it up and the businessman sat down. People laughed, fascinated, as Fofo moved in time with the rhythm, opening and closing his enormous mouth.

Little Chief had watched the show many times. He knew that Papy Bolingô had worked in a circus, in France, during his years of exile. It was doubtless at that time that he'd discovered and developed his extraordinary skills as a ventriloquist, from which he now earned his living.

'Fofo talks!' he would insist, laughing. 'Fofo sings. It's not me. I taught him his first words, he was very little. Then I taught him to sing.'

'Then we want to hear him singing a long way away from you!'

'No chance! That's one thing this guy won't do. He's such a shy little creature.'

Little Chief waited till the end of the show. People were on their way out, really excited, entranced by the miracle they had just witnessed. The businessman approached the performers:

'Congratulations! Better every time.'

'Thanks,' the hippo thanked him with his metallic voice, a dramatic baritone. 'We had a nice audience.'

Little Chief stroked his back:

'How are you getting along, over on your little farm?'

'Very well, *padrinho*. I've got loads of water, and mud for rolling around in.'

Papy Bolingô exploded into bright laughter. His friend

laughed with him. Fofo seemed to imitate them, shaking his head, stamping his thick feet on the little stage.

The owner of the establishment, an old guerilla fighter called Pedro Afonso, had lost his right leg when a landmine exploded. This had not robbed him of his love of dancing. To see him dance, you would never have guessed he wore a prosthesis. He came over, when he heard the two friends laughing, tracing out some ornate rumba steps on the beaten-earth floor:

'God invented music so poor people could be happy.'

He called for beers for the three of them:

'Let's drink to the happiness of the poor.'

Little Chief objected:

'And what about me?'

'You?! Ah yes, I always forget you're rich. Here in our country, the first external sign of wealth is usually arrogance. You don't have any of that about you. The money hasn't gone to your head.'

'Thanks. You know how I became rich?'

'They say a bird came down from the sky, landed in your hand and spat out two diamonds.'

'That's almost how it happened. I killed a pigeon, to eat it, and I found two diamonds in the animal's crop. Just a few days ago I learned whose diamonds they were.' Little Chief was silent a moment, relishing his friends' amazement. 'The diamonds belonged to my neighbour, an old Portuguese lady. She lived in poverty for twenty-something years, despite being rich. And she made me rich – me – without knowing it.'

He told the story, taking time over the details, the twists and turns, inventing whatever he didn't know with talent and relish. Papy Bolingô wanted to know if the old lady had kept some diamonds. Yes, the businessman said. There had been two left, both so big that none of the pigeons wanted them. The Portuguese woman had offered them to a couple of Mucubal shepherds. 'It would seem she knew these hicks, God knows how. Luanda does have its mysteries.'

'True,' Pedro Afonso agreed. 'Our capital is full of mysteries. I've seen things in this city that would be too much even in a dream.'

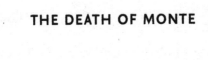

THE DEATH OF MONTE

Magno Moreira Monte was killed by a satellite dish. He fell off the roof while he was trying to fix the aerial. Then the thing fell on his head. Some people saw the events as an ironic allegory for recent times. The former state security agent, the final representative of a past that few in Angola wished to recall, was felled by the future. It was the triumph of free communication over obscurantism, silence and censorship; cosmopolitanism had crushed provincialism.

Maria Clara liked watching the Brazilian soaps. Her husband, meanwhile, took little interest in television. The pointlessness of the programmes infuriated him. The news bulletins made him even angrier. He watched football matches, supporting Primeiro de Agosto and Benfica. From time to time he'd sit down, in pyjamas and slippers, to re-watch some old black-and-white movie or other. He preferred books. He had collected many hundreds of titles. He planned to spend his final years rereading Jorge Amado, Machado de Assis, Clarice Lispector, Luandino Vieira, Ruy Duarte de Carvalho, Julio Cortázar, Gabriel García Márquez.

When they moved house, leaving the dirty, noisy air of the capital behind them, Monte tried to persuade his wife to do without television. Maria Clara agreed. She'd got into the habit of agreeing with him. For the first weeks, they read together. Everything seemed to be going well. But Maria Clara was getting sad. She'd spend hours on the phone with her friends. Monte then decided to buy and install a satellite dish.

Strictly speaking, he died for love.

THE MEETING

THE MEETING

Maria da Piedade Lourenço was a small, nervous woman, with a neglected head of greyish-brown hair that rose up like a crest on the top of her head. Ludo couldn't make out the details of her face. She did, however, notice the crest. She looks like a chicken, she thought, then immediately regretted having thought it. She'd been terribly nervous in the days leading up to her daughter's arrival. But when the woman appeared in front of her, a great calm settled over her. She told her to come in. The living room was painted now and all set up with new flooring, new doors, the whole thing at the expense of her neighbour, Arnaldo Cruz, who had also insisted on giving her furniture. He had bought the apartment from Ludo, granting her lifetime use of it and committing to pay for Sabalu's studies until the boy was done with university.

The woman came in. She sat down on one of the chairs, tense, clinging to her handbag as if to a buoy. Sabalu went to fetch tea and biscuits.

'I'm not sure what I'm supposed to call you.'

'You can call me Ludovica, that's my name.'

'One day will I be able to call you mother?'

Ludo held her hands tight against her belly. Through the windows she could see the highest branches of the mulemba. There was no breeze to disturb them.

'I realise I've got no excuse,' she murmured. 'I was only very young, and I was scared. That doesn't justify what I did.'

Maria da Piedade dragged the chair over to her. She put her right hand on her knee.

'I didn't come to Luanda to claim any debt. I came to meet you. I want to take you back to our country.'

Ludo took her hand.

'This is my country, child. I no longer have any other.' She pointed at the mulemba. 'I've seen that tree grow. It's seen me get old. We've talked a lot.'

'I presume you must have family in Aveiro?'

'Family?'

'Family, friends, whatever.'

Ludo smiled at Sabalu, who was watching it all, very alert, buried in one of the sofas.

'My family is this boy, that mulemba tree out there, and a phantom dog. My eyesight gets worse every day. An ophthalmologist friend of my neighbour was here in the apartment to look at me. He said I would never lose my eyesight completely. I still have my peripheral vision. I'll always be able to make out the light, and the light in this country is a riot. In any case, I don't aspire to any more: the light, Sabalu reading to me, the joy of a pomegranate every day.'

A PIGEON CALLED LOVE

The pigeon that changed Little Chief's life – and also sated his hunger – was called Love. Ridiculous, you think? Take it up with Maria Clara. It was she who gave it the name. The future wife of Magno Moreira Monte was, around the time of Independence, a young high school student. Her father, Horácio Capitão, a customs officer, bred carrier pigeons. Those named by Maria Clara tended to be champions. Before Love, it had been so with Beloved (1968), Amorous (1971), Clamorous (1973) and Enchanted (1973). Love was nearly thrown away while still an egg. 'It's no good,' explained Horácio Capitão to his daughter. 'Look at the shell: crinkled, very thick. A healthy, strong pigeon, a good flyer, is born from an egg with a smooth, bright shell.'

The girl turned the egg around in her long fingers, and prophesied:

'This one's going to be a champion, Dad. I'm going to call it Love.'

Love was born with thin legs. It cheeped a lot in the bowl. Its plumage took a long time to appear. Horácio Capitão didn't hide his displeasure and disgust:

'We ought to get rid of it, Maria Clara. The blasted creature is never going to be a good flyer. It's a loser. A pigeon-keeper needs to know how to distinguish between good pigeons and bad pigeons. The bad ones we get rid of, we don't waste our time on them.'

'No!' his daughter insisted. 'I have complete faith in this pigeon. Love was born to win.'

Love did indeed begin to develop. Unfortunately, it grew too much. Seeing that it was fat, much bigger than the other pigeons from the same brood, Horácio Capitão once again shook his head:

'We should eat it. Big pigeons only have a chance in speed trials. They're no good for long distances.'

He was wrong. Love lived up to Maria Clara's expectations: 1974 and 1975 were glory years, as it proved itself quick and determined, with an ingrained passion for the pigeon house.

'The son of a bitch is demonstrating an attachment to its territory,' Horácio Capitão finally acknowledged. 'Attachment to one's territory is the main characteristic of a good flyer.'

When he stood at the mirror, Horácio Capitão saw a tall, muscular man, which he was not. Quite the contrary, he was barely over a metre sixty, and had scrawny arms, narrow shoulders, little bird-bones. He never shied away from whatever confronted him, and when he had the chance he would throw the first punch, bearing those of his opponent afterwards, bearing them with great suffering on his fragile flesh, but always rigid as a colossus. He had been born in Luanda to a petit bourgeois, mestizo family, and had only visited Portugal once. This fact notwithstanding, he felt himself to be, in his own words,

Portuguese through and through. The April revolution enraged and stunned him. Some days he was more angry, others more stunned, now gazing vacantly into the sky, now railing against the traitors and communists who were planning, shamelessly, to sell Angola to the Soviet Empire. Horrified, he witnessed the start of the civil war and the triumph of the MPLA movement – and of their Cuban allies and the Eastern Bloc. He could have left for Lisbon, like so many others, but he didn't want to:

'As long as there's still a true Portuguese man in this country, Angola will never stop being Portuguese.'

In the months following Independence, he saw the playing out of the tragedies he had prophesied: the flight of the settlers and a good part of the native bourgeoisie, the closing of the factories and small businesses, the collapse of the water and electricity services, as well as the rubbish collection, the mass prisons, the shootings. He stopped spending time at the pigeon house. He spent his days at Biker. 'Didn't I tell you?!' he'd say to the few friends, most of them former civil servants, who still hung around the historic beer hall. He became so irritating, with his repeated insistence on the same old recriminations and the same gloomy premonitions, that after a certain point, the others began referring to him as Didn't-I-Tell-You.

On one of those rainy *cacimbo* mornings he opened the newspaper and saw a photo of a rally. He saw, in the foreground, Maria Clara hugging Magno Moreira Monte, and he ran over to show the paper to a one-time informant of the Portuguese political police, Artur Quevedo, who after Independence would end up doing little odd jobs for the new information and security services.

'Do you know this guy? Who is this guy?'

Quevedo looked at his friend with sympathy.

'He's a fanatical communist. The worst of the communists: smart, determined, with a visceral hatred of the Portuguese.'

Horácio rushed home in a panic. His daughter, his little girl, his princess, had fallen into the hands of a subversive. He didn't know what he'd say to his late wife when he saw her again. His heart sped up as he got closer to the house. His rage began to overcome him. As he opened the front door he was already shouting:

'Maria Clara!'

His daughter came over from the kitchen, wiping her hands on her apron.

'Dad?'

'I want you to start packing your bags. We're going to Lisbon.'

'What?!'

Maria Clara had turned seventeen. She had inherited her mother's tranquil beauty, her father's bravery and stubbornness. Monte, eight years older than her, had been her Portuguese teacher in 1974, the year of the great euphoria. All Horácio's flaws were qualities she admired in Monte. She also allowed herself to be seduced by the low voice in which her teacher, in his classes, used to read the lines from José Régio: *My life is a gale breaking loose. / It's a wave that up-rose. / It is one more atom whose excitement grows… / I don't know where I'm going, / I don't know which way I'm going. – I know I'm not going there!*

The girl took off her apron. She stamped on it, furious.

'You go, then. I'm staying in my country.'

Horácio slapped her.

'You're seventeen years old, and you're my daughter. You do what I tell you. For now you don't leave the house, I won't have you doing anything else stupid.'

He instructed the maid not to let Maria Clara out and he went off to buy plane tickets. He sold the car, for a ridiculous price, to Artur Quevedo and handed him a copy of the keys to the house:

'Go in every day and open the windows, water the garden, so people think it's still being lived in. I don't want the communists occupying the house.'

Maria Clara had for several weeks been using the pigeons to communicate with her lover. Horácio had had the phones disconnected after he'd started receiving anonymous calls and death threats. These threats weren't connected to any political business. Nothing to do with that. The customs officer suspected some jealous colleague. Monte, meanwhile, travelled a lot, carrying out secret missions, sometimes in combat zones. Maria Clara, who at this point was taking sole care of the pigeon house, would give him three or four pigeons, which he would release, at twilight, with love verses and brief pieces of news tied to their legs.

Maria Clara managed to send, via the maid, a message to a girlfriend, who went off to find Monte. She found him in Viana, investigating rumours about the planning of a military coup involving black officers who were discontented with the prevalence of whites and mestizos at the highest levels of the armed forces. Monte sat down and wrote:

Tomorrow. Six o'clock, usual place. Be very careful. I love you.

He put the message into a little plastic cylinder and fixed it to the right leg of one of the two pigeons he had brought with him. He released the pigeon.

Maria Clara waited in vain for a reply. She cried all night. She made no protest on the way to the airport. She didn't say a word until they had disembarked in Lisbon. But she didn't stay long in the Portuguese capital. Five months after turning eighteen she returned to Luanda and married Monte. Horácio swallowed his pride, packed his bags and followed his daughter. He would learn, much later, that his future son-in-law had several times prevented his being thrown in prison, in the stormy years after Independence. He never thanked him. At his funeral, however, he was one of those who shed the most tears.

God weighs souls on a pair of scales. In one of the dishes is the soul, and in the other, the tears of those who weep for it. If nobody cries, the soul goes down to Hell. If there are enough tears, and they are sufficiently heartfelt, it rises up to Heaven. Ludo believed this. Or wanted to believe this. That was what she told Sabalu:

'People who are missed by other people, they are the ones who go to Paradise. Paradise is the space we occupy in other people's hearts. That's what my grandmother used to tell me. I don't believe it. I'd like to believe in anything that's so simple – but I lack faith.'

Monte had people to cry for him. I find it hard to imagine him in Paradise. Perhaps, however, he's being purged in some obscure nook of immensity, between the serene splendour of Heaven and the twisted darkness of Hell, playing chess with the angels who are guarding him. If the angels know how to play, if they play well, this would be almost Paradise to him.

As for Horácio Capitão, old Didn't-I-Tell-You, he spends his afternoons in a rundown bar on Ilha, drinking beer and arguing about politics, in the company of the poet Vitorino Gavião, Artur Quevedo, and another two or three aged cadavers from the old days. To this day he doesn't recognise Angola's Independence. He believes that just as communism ended, so one day Independence will end, too. He still breeds pigeons.

the angels who are guarding him. If the angels knew how to play, if they play well, this would be almost Paradise to him. As for Horacio Capitán old 'Didn't-I-Tell-You', he spends his afternoons in a rundown bar on, that, drinking beer and singing about politics, in the company of the poet Vicertio Clavis, Arturo Quevedo, and another two or three aged fellows from the old days. To this day he doesn't recognise Augusto's independence. He believes that, just as communism ended, so one day independence will end, too. He still breeds pigeons.

THE CONFESSION OF
JEREMIAS CARRASCO

Let us return to the morning when Nasser Evangelista, overcome by the echo of dark voices, hurled himself at Monte and stabbed him. Amid the confusion of people gathering at Ludo's door, there were two characters in black, as you might recall, who stood out. The old lady noticed them after Monte's shameful flight and the (also hurried) exit of Baiacu. She noticed them, but had no way of knowing what they had come for since, in the meantime, Daniel Benchimol had begun to read the letter that Maria da Piedade Lourenço had written to the managing director of the *Jornal de Angola.*

The two men waited for the journalist to finish. They bore silent witness to Ludo's anguish, to the tears wiped away with the back of her hand. Finally Daniel withdrew, promising to write to Maria da Piedade, and the two men stepped forward. The older of the two held out his hand to Ludo, but it was the younger who spoke:

'May we come in, auntie?'

'What do you want?'

Jeremias Carrasco took a notebook from his jacket pocket

and wrote something quickly in it. He showed it to Ludo. The woman shook her head:

'I can see it's a notebook. I can't read the letters any more. Are you a mute?'

The young man read aloud:

'Let us in – please. I need your forgiveness, and your help.'

Ludo faced up to them, obstinately:

'I have nowhere for you to sit. It's been thirty years since I've had visitors.'

Jeremias wrote again, then showed the notebook to his son:

'We'll stand. My father says that chairs, even the best ones, don't improve conversations.'

Ludo let them in. Sabalu went to fetch four old oilcans. They sat down on them. Jeremias looked in horror at the cement floor, the dark walls scratched in charcoal. He took off his hat. His shaved skull shone in the gloom. He wrote again in his notebook.

'Your sister and brother-in-law died in a car accident,' read the son. 'It was my fault. I killed them. I met Spike in Uíge, at the start of the war. He was the one who sought me out. Someone told him about me. He needed my help to run a sting on the Diamang mining company. A good clean job, done well, with no blood spilled and no confusion. We agreed that I'd keep half the stones. I did what I had to do, it all worked out, but at the last minute old Spike ran off. I was left empty-handed. He never thought I'd come after him to Luanda. He didn't know me. I travelled into the city, which was surrounded by Mobutu's troops and our own people, a crazy venture, and by looking

228

here and there, within a couple of days, I found him at a party on Ilha. He fled as soon as he saw me. I chased after him in my car, like in the movies. Then he went off the road and crashed into a tree. Your sister died at once. Spike lived long enough to tell me where he'd hidden the diamonds. I'm very sorry.'

António read with some difficulty. Perhaps because of the lack of light, perhaps because he wasn't used to reading, perhaps because it was hard for him to believe what the words said. When he'd finished he looked up at his father, amazement in his eyes. The old man was leaning back against the wall. He was having trouble breathing. He took the notebook from António's hands and wrote again. Ludo raised her hand in a vague, agonised gesture, trying to prevent him:

'Don't torture yourself any more. Our mistakes correct us. Perhaps we need to forget. We should practise forgetting, reaching for oblivion.'

Jeremias shook his head, irritated. He scribbled a few more words in the little notebook. He handed it to his son.

'My father doesn't want to forget. Forgetting is dying, he says. Forgetting is surrender.'

The old man wrote again.

'My father is asking me to talk about my people. He wants me to tell you about the oxen, the oxen are our wealth, but they're not goods for buying and selling. We like to hear the cries of the oxen.'

In his isolation among the Mucubals, Jeremias had been reborn not as another person, but as many – as another people. Before then he had been surrounded by others. At the very best, he was an individual with his arms around others. In the desert, he felt for the first time as though he were a part of it all. Some biologists argue that a single bee, a single ant, is nothing more than the mobile cells of one individual. The true organisms are the beehive and the ant nest. A Mucubal, too, can exist only with others.

As António struggled to read his father's explanations, Ludo recalled some lines from Fernando Pessoa: *I feel sorry for the stars / Which have shined for so long, / So long, so long... / I feel sorry for the stars. // Is there not a weariness / Felt by things, / By all things, / Such as we feel in our limbs? // A weariness of existing, / Of being, / Just of being, / Whether sad or happy... // Is there not, finally, / For all things that are, / Not just death / But some other finality? / Or a higher purpose, / Some kind of pardon?*

António was talking about the new landowners, about the barbed wire that divided up the desert, cutting off the access paths to the pastures. Responding with gunfire led to terrible wars, in which the Mucubals lost their cattle, they lost their souls, their liberty. That's how it had been in 1940, when the Portuguese killed almost all the people, sending the survivors as slaves to the São Tomé plantations. The alternative solution, according to Jeremias, would be to buy land, the same land that once belonged to the Kuvale, the Himba, the Muchavicua, and which today belongs to generals and wealthy businessmen, many of whom have no connection to the vast southern sky.

Ludo got up, went to fetch the two diamonds that were left, and handed them over to Jeremias.

THE ACCIDENT

Often, when I used to look in a mirror, I'd see him behind me. I no longer do. Perhaps because I see so poorly now (a benefit of blindness), perhaps because we've replaced the mirrors. As soon as the money for the apartment came in, I bought new mirrors. I got rid of the old ones. My neighbour found this strange:

'The only things in decent condition in your apartment are the mirrors.'

'No!' I got annoyed. 'The mirrors are haunted!'

'Haunted?!'

'That's right, dear neighbour. They're full of shadows. They've spent too long in a state of solitude.'

I didn't want to tell him that often, when I looked into the mirrors, I saw looming over me the man who raped me. In those days I still used to leave the house. I led an almost normal life. I'd go to and from school, by bicycle. In the summer we'd rent a house on the Costa Nova. I'd go swimming. I liked swimming. One afternoon, as we arrived home from the beach, I realised I was missing the book I'd been reading. I went back, alone, to find it. There was a row of little beach huts set up on the sand. It was getting dark now, though, and they were deserted. I headed for the hut we'd been using. I went in. I heard a noise, and as I turned I saw a man standing at the door, smiling at me. I recognised him. I used to see him, in a bar, playing cards with my father. I was going to explain what I was doing there, but I didn't get the chance. As I was about to speak he was already on top of me. He tore my dress, ripped my knickers, and penetrated me. I remember the smell. And his hands, rough, hard, squeezing my breasts. I screamed. He slapped my face, hard, rhythmic blows, not with hatred, not angrily, as though he were enjoying himself. I fell silent. I arrived home sobbing, my dress torn, covered in blood, my face swollen. My father understood everything. He went out of his mind. He slapped me. As he lashed me, with his belt, he screamed at me. Whore, tramp, wretch! I can still hear him today. Whore! Whore! My mother clinging to him. My sister in tears.

I never knew for sure what happened to the man who raped me. He was a fisherman. They say he ran off to Spain. He disappeared. I became pregnant. I locked myself away in a bedroom. They locked me away in a bedroom. Outside, I heard people whispering. When it was time, a midwife came to help me. I never even saw my daughter's face. They took her from me.

                                                                      The shame.

The shame is what stopped me leaving the house. My father died without ever addressing another word to me. I would go into the living room and he'd get up and leave. Years passed, he died. Some months later, my mother followed him. I moved to my sister's house. Bit by bit I forgot myself. I thought about my child every day. Every day I taught myself not to think about her.

I was never again able to go out without feeling a profound shame.

That has passed, now. I go out and I no longer feel ashamed. I no longer feel afraid. I go out and the grocer women greet me. They give me a laugh, as though we are family.

The children play with me, they take my hand. I don't know if it's because I'm very old, or because I'm as much a child as they are.

LAST WORDS

LAST WORDS

I write feeling my way through the letters. An odd experience, as I cannot read what I have written. Therefore, I am not writing for myself.

For whom am I writing?

I am writing for the person I used to be. Perhaps the person I once left behind persists, standing there, still and grim, in some attic of time – on a bend, at a crossroads – and in some mysterious way she is able to read the lines I am setting out here, without seeing them.

Ludo, my dear: I am happy now.

Blind as I am, I see better than you. I weep for your blindness, for your infinite stupidity. It would have been so easy for you to open the door, so easy for you to go into the street and embrace life. I see you peering out of the window, terrified, like a child peeping under the bed expecting to find monsters.

Monsters, show me the monsters: these people out on the street.

My people.

I'm so sorry for everything you've missed.

So sorry.

But isn't unhappy humanity just like you?

DREAMS ARE WHERE IT ALL BEGINS

In her dreams, Ludo was a little girl. She was sitting on a beach of white sand. Sabalu, lying on his back, his head in her lap, was looking at the sea. They were talking about the past and the future. They were exchanging recollections. They laughed over the strange way they'd met. The laugh that came from the two of them shook the air, like a dazzle of birds in the sleepy morning. Then, Sabalu got up:

'The day is born, Ludo. Let's go.'

And they went, the two of them, towards the light, laughing and talking, like two people about to head out to sea.

Lisbon, 5 February 2012

ACKNOWLEDGEMENTS
AND BIBLIOGRAPHY

On a now distant afternoon back in 2004, the filmmaker Jorge António challenged me to write the screenplay for a feature-length film to be shot in Angola. I told him the story of a Portuguese woman who bricked herself in, just days before Independence in 1975, terrified by the way events were progressing. Thanks to Jorge's enthusiasm, I did write the screenplay. Although the film fell by the wayside, it was from that original structure that I came to this novel. In order to write the chapters about the Kuvale, I found some inspiration in the poems of Ruy Duarte de Carvalho, as well as in one of his most brilliant essays: 'Aviso à Navegação: A brief introductory look at the Kuvale shepherds', INALD, Luanda, 1997.

Several people have helped me in the writing of this book. I would like to thank, in particular, my parents, who have always been my first readers, as well as Patrícia Reis and Lara Longle. Finally, I would like to thank the Brazilian poet Christiana Nóvoa, who at my request wrote Ludo's poems in the chapters 'Haikai' and 'Exorcism'.

penguin.co.uk/vintage